TWO DOWN

"Engaging." —*Publishers Weekly*

"*Two Down* is as entertaining as the series debut. . . . Fun. Readers who enjoy a different type of who-done-it starring two likable characters and six puzzles will fully relish Mr. Blanc's latest across-and-down novel." —*Bookbrowser.com*

THE CROSSWORD MURDER

"Addicts of crossword puzzles will relish *The Crossword Murder*. . . . Treat yourself to a pleasant diversion." —*Chicago Sun-Times*

"Evoe! At last puzzle fans have their revenge . . . super sleuthing and solving for puzzle lovers and mystery fans." —Charles Preston, Puzzle Editor, *USA Today*

"A puzzle lover's delight. . . . A touch of suspense, a pinch of romance, and a whole lot of clever word clues. Blanc has concocted a story sure to appeal to crossword addicts and mystery lovers alike. What's a three-letter word for this book? F-U-N." —Earlene Fowler, author of *Arkansas Traveler*

"Designed to delight. . . . Adroit word play and high society intrigue . . . an enjoyable, complex solution and likable protagonists. . . . Clever." —*Publishers Weekly*

"Good summer entertainment." —*Philadelphia City Paper*

THE
CROSSWORD
CONNECTION

NERO BLANC

BERKLEY PRIME CRIME, NEW YORK

This is a work of fiction. Names, characters, places, and incidents either are the product of the author's imagination or are used fictitiously, and any resemblance to actual persons, living or dead, business establishments, events, or locales is entirely coincidental.

THE CROSSWORD CONNECTION

A Berkley Prime Crime Book / published by arrangement with the authors

PRINTING HISTORY
Berkley Prime Crime trade paperback edition / July 2001
Berkley Prime Crime mass-market edition / August 2002

Copyright © 2001 by Cordelia Frances Biddle and Steve Zettler.
Cover art by Grace Devito.
Cover design by Judy Murello.

Visit our website at
www.penguinputnam.com

ISBN 0-425-18579-6

Berkley Prime Crime Books are published by
The Berkley Publishing Group,
a division of Penguin Putnam Inc.,
375 Hudson Street, New York, New York 10014.
The name BERKLEY PRIME CRIME and the
BERKLEY PRIME CRIME design
are trademarks belonging to Penguin Putnam Inc.

PRINTED IN THE UNITED STATES OF AMERICA

10 9 8 7 6 5 4 3 2 1

For
Natalee Rosenstein
with much
affection & appreciation

A character in *The Crossword Connection*
was donated to benefit the Alzheimer's
Association of Southeastern Pennsylvania

"A dead man cannot bite."
—Gnaeus Pompeius

CHAPTER

1

"See anything yet?" The older man didn't look up from his newspaper; at this point, he wasn't even bothering to peer over his plastic, fourteen-dollar drugstore reading glasses. It was getting late, and he was beginning to think the entire night would pan out to be a complete bust.

"It's too dark. Let me turn on the headlights for a second, will ya? I mean, how're they even gonna know we're here waitin' for 'em otherwise?"

"You turn the lights on, I smash your brains all over the dashboard. I mean that. I don't want them to know we got a car. If they know we got money, we're in trouble. . . . They'll want to negotiate." He tossed the entertainment section of the *Evening Crier* onto the Cadillac's rear seat, switched off a pocket-sized flashlight, and threw his pencil and glasses into the glove compartment. "Somebody ought to kill that babe. They'd be doin' all of Newcastle, Mass., a big friggin' favor."

"What are you talkin' about?"

"What do you mean, 'What am I talkin' about'?"

"You didn't tell me we was here to kill some babe. You said we was here to—"

The older man sighed in irritation. "How come you never pay even a little bit of attention? What do you think I've been doin' for the last two hours plus that we been waitin' for these guys?"

The younger man paused. He stared straight ahead into the pitch-black alley, then glanced at his partner's faintly illumined face, and finally turned toward the car's rear seat. "The crosswords." The words were mumbled as if he were fearful of responding to a trick question.

"Keerecto! And who's the crosswords dame at the *Crier*?"

Instead of replying, the younger man merely gripped the steering wheel tighter.

"What a friggin' dummy!" his partner swore. "Belle Graham, that's who."

"We gotta off her?"

The older man shifted angrily in his seat, his bony knees scraping the glove compartment. "Get a grip, will ya?"

"But you just said—"

"It was an expression, all right? Like 'I'd kill for a piece of that pie. . . . ' " Anticipating that the next query would probably be "What kind of pie?" the aggrieved tone continued. "Look, the friggin' puzzle gets harder as the week progresses. Wednesday's tougher than Tuesday's . . . like that. By the time Friday, Saturday rolls around, you gotta be a friggin' Einstein. I don't even buy the friggin' paper that late in the week."

"Then how do you know what the Red Sox are doin'?"

The older man's voice almost exploded. "I got a TV, you know."

His partner remained silent for a long moment. In the dim light, his face was contorted with thought. "You want some help? Is that what you're sayin'?"

"Don't make me laugh. . . . Ya gotta have smarts. . . . I mean who the hell knows what the capital of Oregon is, huh?"

"Salem," was the quiet answer.

The older man gave the younger one a long, hard stare, then reached a thin arm toward the discarded newspaper. "You sure?"

"We memorized all the capitals in seventh grade. . . . Mrs. Northrop, the teacher? She made us."

"Well, now, that's *exactly* what I mean. We got a friggin' Salem right here in Massachusetts. Why's this dame makin' a reference to some state nobody's ever heard of?"

The younger man made a sudden, silencing gesture with his right hand. "What's that?"

"What?"

"Over there." His fingers pointed through the Cadillac's windshield at a dark figure walking slowly toward them.

Both men slid down until only their eyes and the tops of their heads were visible. "Looks like a bum from how he's dressed," the older partner whispered.

"Yeah, but he's got something under his coat. See? In his right hand? What is that? Do you think it's the package?"

The men watched in silence as their surprise visitor continued to move through the alley. "There was supposed to be two people . . . brothers or somethin' . . . not bums like that. They got plenty of dough—"

"What if this street guy stole the package from them . . . or maybe, he's like their bagman?"

"Wise up! These guys are pros. That's why they like

dealin' with pros like you and me. You think they're gonna let some *vagrant* get the drop on them and boost the package? No way, José."

"All's I'm sayin' is, maybe we should find out what the guy's got under his coat. That's all I'm sayin', okay?"

"Bottle of Sneaky Pete, probably. What time ya got?"

The younger man glanced at his watch. "Two-thirty-three."

"What's the creep doing now?"

"He turned down Adams Alley. You want we should both get out and follow him?"

The older man hesitated. "I don't know, let me think here. Where's that alley go? Is it a dead end?"

"Nah, it goes through to Seventh Street."

The men sat quietly for another few minutes while the older partner worked out a plan. Eventually, he reached into the glove compartment, removed a .22 caliber automatic pistol, and placed it on his lap. "Okay, here's what we do. You follow the old guy . . . find out what he's carrying. If it's the package, grab it. I'll stay here with the car in case we gotta get the hell outta here."

"You want me to go down that alley alone?"

"There's no one down there but that *vagrant*. Waddya afraid of?"

"Nothin'. I just don't want the guy to make me."

"If he makes you . . . you do him. What's one dead street guy? Nobody's gonna miss him; that's for sure."

This rationale seemed to make sense to both partners. The younger man slid from behind the Cadillac's steering wheel and trotted across Eighth Street to the entrance of Adams Alley. He looked back once before disappearing in the darkness. In the car, his partner checked to see that his automatic pistol had a round in the chamber. Then he removed the safety and placed the gun on the dashboard.

Time seemed to pass slowly, but in reality it was only thirty seconds before a set of headlights, deep within Adams Alley, sprang to sudden life. The younger man was caught in the light as the sound of screeching tires pierced the air. When the car bore down on him, he turned and fled toward the Cadillac, where his waiting partner had made a dive for the floor.

In another thirty seconds, the mysterious vehicle had spun past the Cadillac and disappeared. "Did you see that?" the younger man demanded as his friend reappeared. "The creep tried to run me over! Missed me by a damn inch . . . if that."

The older man tucked the pistol into his belt and stepped from the car. He looked around to see if the fracas had attracted any attention, but the scene was as dark and quiet as before. "How many guys in the car?"

"The damn headlights near blinded me. . . . Two, I think . . . Hell, I don't know—"

"What make?"

"Ford, Chevy . . . Couldn't tell."

"Well, what color was it?"

"I didn't see. Tan maybe. The headlights were high up, though . . . like them SUVs. But—"

"Those two brothers we been waitin' for, probably . . . They're just the type to drive one of them things. . . . Come on." He pulled the pistol from his belt and walked toward Adams Alley.

"Where're ya goin'?"

"I'm gonna see what the hell that street creep had on him. I'm tired of playin' games here."

CHAPTER

2

"What a mess."

Lieutenant Al Lever lit a cigarette and waited for the match to cool. When it had, he placed the warm cardboard-and-sulfur-ash stick into his jacket pocket. The last thing he wanted was to litter one of his own crime scenes. He glanced again at the bloodied and lifeless form at his feet and shook his head. "Any ID?"

Lever directed the question to Patrolman Wallace, the uniformed police officer who'd discovered the body.

"Nothing turned up, Lieutenant. But from the looks of him, I'd have to guess he's from Father Tom's Saint Augustine Mission down near Congress and Water Streets. Definitely a hand-me-down suit. The moths had a field day with it."

"Money?"

"None. Guess he could have been robbed, but he doesn't look like the kind of guy who was rolling in cash. I'd say he hadn't shaved in a good two weeks."

"Did you ask around? Anybody see anything?"

Out of reflex, Wallace glanced at his watch. He gave Lever a slight shrug. "It's five A.M., lieutenant. . . . There's not a soul awake for three square blocks, and no telling when the last person entered this alley . . . besides our victim, here. No one walks here after nightfall. I only patrol once a night myself, and I'll bet I haven't passed a single pedestrian in the last three years." His eyes moved to the dead man. "And once this bit of good news hits the *Evening Crier*, I'd say Adams Alley's going to be off limits for the citizens of Newcastle for another three years."

"Any sign of Jones?" Lever asked, referring to the department's forensics expert.

"Yes, sir. Mr. Jones got here almost an hour ago. Finished up his preliminary and scooted off for a cup of coffee. Said he'd be right back."

Lever took a long pull from his cigarette and coughed spasmodically as he blew the smoke from his lungs. His growing paunch rolled with the movement, and his starched yellow shirt reflected a pallid green in the predawn light. In the coastal Massachusetts city, early May mornings were cool.

Jones approached with three covered blue and white coffee containers. Steam, like whale spouts, puffed from the slits in the plastic lids. "Figured you'd be here by now," he said as he handed a coffee cup to Lever and another to Wallace, who produced a small salute of thanks. Lever nodded and coughed.

"You know what they say about those cancer sticks, don't you, Al?"

Between a few more coughs, Lever said, "No, Abe, what do they say about cancer sticks? Thanks for the java, by the way."

"No problemo. They say they give you cancer; that's what they say."

"Thank you *so* much, *Dr.* Jones, for that invaluable piece of information. However, I don't need a man with a degree in forensic pathology to remind me. It says so right on the damn pack. It has for years."

"Then someone should teach you how to read, Al."

"You're a riot, Abe. Handsome *and* witty. The Newcastle Police Department is truly blessed."

Jones chortled. "The right kind of exercise, Al. That's all you need for a physique like mine."

"Right."

The three men sucked at their coffee cups. In the cool, dim light, Jones's teeth shone like bright, white neon. Lever was right; Absalom "Abe" Jones was far and away the best-looking man in the police department, as many women in Newcastle could attest. A solid six feet, and bearing a strong resemblance to a youthful Harry Belafonte, Abe took enormous pleasure in baiting his boss. He mocked an exaggerated yawn. "Man, I'll tell ya, I got no sleep at all last night."

"I don't want to hear about it, Abe."

"Some women just don't know when to stop, if you know what I mean. Ever been with a lady like that, Al?"

Lever coughed again. "Spare us, please. For your information, I didn't get any sleep last night either." His coughing jag increased. "Damn allergies. They kept me up all night."

"Springtime, Al. The birds and the bees and pollen all over the place."

The lieutenant chuckled. Then he brought his gaze back to the body in the alley. His face went sour. "I don't like this situation, Abe."

"You're not supposed to like it. A man's dead. Why would you like it?"

"I mean, look at this poor schmo. What'd he have going for him? And to end up like this? A wasted life, if you ask me."

"We don't know that. To begin with, we don't have positive identification. He could've been a doctor or a judge at one point. It wouldn't be the first time an educated person hit the skids. . . . Things get out of control, and it can be a long spiral down."

Lever sighed, walked the thirty feet to where Adams Alley met Seventh Street, stubbed out his cigarette on a wall, and carefully put the remainder in his pocket. He watched as an early morning crosstown bus pushed east. He then ambled back to the dead man. "So, Abe, what did you turn up with your preliminary?"

"The crime appears to be pretty cut and dried." Jones pointed to a plastic bag containing a rectangular piece of granite. "You see this cobblestone? There are clear traces of blood and matted hair. I'm assuming that this is your murder weapon. Someone slammed it into the victim's skull . . . once, only . . . from my initial examination. I'll dust the weapon and that liquor bottle over there for prints, pick up those stray cigar butts, and pull DNA samples. But that's about it. Nothing else appears out of the ordinary. . . . Nothing that doesn't belong to a back alley. Well, there are some tire marks up closer to Eighth Street." He pointed casually. "I'll check them out, but I'm not optimistic they're connected."

Lever sighed but didn't speak. He kept his hands in his pockets.

"Hey . . . Al . . . It happens all the time, all across America. These homeless guys get liquored up, fight over a bottle, and one of them ends up clobbering the other. Sooner or later, the person who did this will walk into your office and spill his guts so that he can get a dry place to sleep and three squares for the rest of his life."

"Yeah, but if your scenario's correct, where are the signs of a struggle? I'm looking, but I don't see any. There's the guy's bed, a comfy nest of newspapers. He props up his head with the comics section and drifts off into dreamland. People arguing over a bottle don't die peacefully in bed. We don't even have a little broken glass here."

"Being hit in the head with a fifteen-pound lump of stone isn't exactly a peaceful death, Al. Besides, motive's your department, not mine. Maybe our victim stole the pint of booze, and the former owner came after him. Found the bottle empty—which it is—and nailed the thief in his sleep. Tempers often run short among these marginal types, especially when they're hoarding something important."

Lever thought. He turned his attention to Wallace. "Nothing remotely valuable on the body?"

"Not in immediate evidence, sir. Maybe the ME will turn up something interesting during the autopsy."

Lever took another swig of his coffee. "Something's really wrong here."

Abe Jones gave him a comradely grin. "You need a day off, Al. That's all."

"The guy went to sleep on *Peanuts,* for Pete's sake. You know, Charlie Brown, Snoopy . . ."

"Speaking of Snoopy, Wallace found dog food in the victim's pockets."

"What?"

Wallace answered, "That's right, sir. Three small cans;

the kind with snap-off lids. A fourth empty can containing a plastic fork sat beside the body."

Lever let out another weary sigh.

Jones touched his shoulder. "A homeless guy on a binge, Al. What else can you say? He was reduced to eating dog food. . . . They say cat food tastes like tuna. Dog food . . . I don't know. I hope I never have to find out."

"Poor schmo."

Patrolman Wallace interrupted them. "Carlyle's here with the morgue wagon, Lieutenant. Looks like he wants to back it down the alley."

Lever glanced at Jones for approval.

"Sure, tell him it's okay," Abe said. "But ask him to stay back fifteen feet until I finish processing."

Lever watched in silence as Newcastle's dark gray morgue wagon eased down the alley. The steady beep-beep of the reverse warning signal pierced the cool morning air, bouncing off the empty industrial buildings, the fire escapes, and grungy, broken windows. Eventually, the van came to a halt, and the noise subsided. Carlyle, the medical examiner, stepped from the passenger's side, slipping on latex surgical gloves as he did.

"What have we got?"

Lever spoke. "Dead John Doe, no ID. See what you can piece together. I'll need a time of death. Not that it'll do much good. . . ." His words trailed off.

"Uh-oh." Carlyle looked at Jones. "Do we have a depressed lieutenant on our hands?"

"He just doesn't like to see Charlie Brown bloodied up. Reminds him of his own mortality."

Carlyle gave Jones a thin smile as he bent down to examine the body. "I'd say this guy's been dead for two or three hours. Maybe longer, judging from the dried blood.

But then again, newspaper can often soak up blood more rapidly than cloth. I won't be able to supply an exact time until I perform an autopsy. He didn't suffer, if that makes you feel better, Al. This was quick, and definitely premeditated. Someone didn't like this guy. If he was a mobster, we'd be calling it a hit."

Lever and Jones watched as Carlyle finished the prelim. He made notations on a form attached to a stainless steel clipboard; when he'd finished, his driver appeared with a black plastic body bag. He and Carlyle placed the victim in it, zipped it up, then positioned the bag on a stretcher, which they wheeled into the morgue van. Carlyle closed the van's doors and turned to Lever.

"I'll try to get the information by noon, Al. This alley gives me the chills. . . . Always has."

"It's just an alleyway."

Carlyle looked at Lever. "It's not a place I'd walk down at night."

After the van disappeared, Lever and Jones studied the saturated newspapers. The blood was still sticky where the body had been; in other spots, it was dry.

"Have you ever known anything to give Carlyle the chills?" Lever asked somewhat rhetorically. "Penguins get more chills than he does."

Jones chuckled, "He's an odd one, all right. . . . Hmmm, this is interesting."

"What's that?"

"Look at the papers. John Doe used a local newspaper, the *Evening Crier*, to sleep on. But his head rested on the *Boston Sentinel*."

"He probably pulled whatever he could find out of the recycling bin over there." Lever cocked his head toward a large wheeled plastic cart. It was piled high with discarded newspapers and magazines with a number of empty bottles and cans semisubmerged in the morass. A garbagey odor rose from the container, and a furtive scuffle indicated the stealthy presence of rats. "Or, maybe he likes the comics. The ones in the *Crier* stink. They never did have *Peanuts*."

"I'll see if I can lift some prints from the paper bin."

Lever stared at the blood-soaked papers. "Right. Whatever you do, Abe, don't chuck these babies back inside it. Might not sit well with the neighbors."

CHAPTER

3

"The word begins with a *C*," Belle said gently, "not a *K*." She pointed to the lined-paper practice notebook the other woman was laboring over. It was full of snippets of poetry, beginnings of stories, phrases heard and jotted down, and sidebar doodles that reflected a hidden artistic talent.

"Like in Sister Mary Catherine?"

"Exactly, Rayanne! Just like Sister Mary Catherine!" Belle gave her student's shoulder a quick, affectionate pat. "Courage," she said. "C-O-U-R-A-G-E. The word has *heart* at its center. Two thousand years ago, in what is now Italy, *cor* meant heart."

Rayanne stared at the notebook. "How'd you get to know stuff like that? Is it on accounta you working at the newspaper?"

Belle considered her answer. She and Rayanne were both in their early thirties: two healthy women of medium height and slender build whose only outward physical difference was that Rayanne had brown hair and Belle was a blond. Technically, they should have had equality in choices and careers, but their dual backgrounds had obviously presented such a disparity of opportunities that it was only Belle Graham who had learned that education mattered, and only Belle who had been taught to value self-respect and pride.

"I know about language, Rayanne, because it fascinates me, and I've worked hard studying it. The same way you work on your poetry and all those stories you've begun."

Rayanne's face clouded with an old habit of frustration and anxiety. "But I can't spell like—"

Belle's gray eyes smiled. "I'll tell you a secret, Ray. Spelling's not nearly as important as the emotions you intuit and experience. . . . All the thoughts you've expressed in your notebook."

"I can't get a job if I can't spell. That's what Sister Mary Catherine says."

"Well, she's right. That's why you and I are working together."

"You gonna make me do crossword puzzles like the ones you put in the newspaper?" Rayanne asked this in jest, and Belle just as lightheartedly responded, "I'm not about to force you to do anything you don't want. Besides, Ray, you'd win hands down. My idea of exercise is picking up a dictionary."

"Brains and brawn, you and me."

Belle grinned. "You know what you've got there, Ray? Alliteration. Two words with repeated consonants . . . similar sounds."

"Fear and beer . . . beaten, cheatin' . . ."

Belle hesitated. Her students' struggles and life stories often came out in unexpected ways. "Those are rhymes actually, Ray. Did you put them in your new poem?"

Seated side by side at cast-off school desks, the women returned to Rayanne's notebook. As a volunteer with the Margaret House Shelter, the women's counterpart to Father Tom's Saint Augustine Mission for Men, Belle had quickly discovered that her efforts at teaching literacy fared better if the students' own words were used. Encouraged to write autobiographies or fiction, the women had ownership of the letters on the page. And ownership, Belle knew from experience, was empowerment.

"What's that Italian word for heart again, Belle?"

"*Cor.* It's Latin. That was the language of Italy then. Just as you and I are speaking English. Or some folks around here speak Portuguese or Spanish or Greek. Then *cor* evolved into *cuer,* an old French word that's become *coeur* today. But even before *cor,* there was the ancient Greek *kardia,* which gives us the root for cardiac—"

Rayanne's pencil flew in the air. "You're giving me cardiac arrest!"

Belle beamed. "You've got it!"

It was then that the shelter's director, Sister Mary Catherine, walked into the room. She was in her midsixties, a person of indefatigable energy and zeal who had grown up on a Navajo Indian reservation in Arizona, been educated by nuns, taken vows herself, then devoted her life to teaching the most impoverished in the nation before moving to Newcastle and beginning a new career at the shelter she and Sister Zoe had helped establish. "This city!" she said, sinking heavily in a nearby chair. It was an uncharacteristic gesture of weariness and defeat.

Rayanne looked at her, immediately nervous and fearful. She bit her lip and curled her gnawed fingertips into her palms. "They gonna get the building, ain't they, Sister?"

"Not if I can help it." Sister Mary Catherine forced a

tight smile, then deftly changed the subject. "How's our star pupil?"

"Creating alliterations and rhymes," Belle answered. "And a super poem about courage."

Sister Mary Catherine nodded, but her mouth remained grim, the only discordant element in an otherwise grandmotherly demeanor.

"Is it the Peterman brothers?" Rayanne asked.

The nun paused before speaking. Belle could see her weighing how much information to share with one of the mission residents and then deciding that knowledge was the first stepping-stone to responsibility. "Yes, it's the Peterman brothers, Rayanne, plus a close friend of theirs who sits on the City Council. . . . Also a Canadian real estate enterprise, some female venture capitalist from New York . . . and that's only the folks that have come forward publicly.

"When Father Tom established the Saint Augustine Mission and Sister Zoe and I started Margaret House, who knew that this part of Newcastle would become a 'hot property'? I've actually seen the loft building across the street listed just that way in a real estate advertisement. 'Hot property' indeed." She turned to Belle. "Oh, yes, I've heard the hateful rumors those money grubbers have been spreading. The shelters 'attract undesirables'; we 'encourage the criminal element'. Give me a break! God and Mammon: No man can serve two masters."

"They're not gonna make us move, are they?" Rayanne's tone had dropped to a fierce whisper.

"Over my dead body," was Sister Mary Catherine's angry reply. Then her weathered face broke into a smile of genuine warmth. "How's the almost bride?"

"Eight days left." Belle tried to match the nun's determinedly jovial demeanor. She glanced at her watch. "Eight

days, seven hours, and fifty-two minutes until Annabella
Graham weds one Rosco Polycrates. But who's counting? . . . Oh, geez, I didn't realize it was so late. I told
Rosco's sister Cleo I'd stop by and look at her kitchen renovation; then he and I are getting the all-important
license. . . . I've got to go, Ray. See you Monday."

"Brains and brawn," Rayanne replied.

"It's not either/or, Ray. You've got to give yourself
credit."

"Fight. Right," Ray said.

D riving to Rosco's sister's suburban home, Belle was
subjected to the usual conflicting emotions she experienced after leaving the shelter. There was no doubt that
the two nuns who ran the mission were remarkable people.
There was also no doubt that many of the residents had
wonderful and untapped gifts and that enthusiastic support
was all they needed to get their lives back on track: finish
educations, find and keep jobs, discover self-worth.

The problem lay in the fact that for each woman who
successfully passed through and out of the system, another
appeared at the door. How Sister Mary Catherine and Sister Zoe lived with this dilemma while maintaining a sanguine outlook was something Belle didn't understand,
especially now that they were facing so much pressure
from the city's business interests. An ordinance declaring
residential shelters illegal in the area wasn't out of the
realm of possibility.

Pondering these myriad problems, Belle turned her car
into Cleo's drive, swerved to avoid a jumble of neighborhood children's bikes, parked, walked up to the entry,
sidestepping a baseball bat, a soccer ball, a pint-sized foot-

ball helmet, and two water pistols as large and black as military rifles.

She rang the doorbell and was greeted by the sound of dogs barking, kids bounding up and down the stairs, the whine of a masonry saw, and the rhythmic pounding of a hammer. Belle knocked, waited, then opened the door and edged into the living room. "Cleo? Hello? It's me, Belle."

A year-old basset hound running sideways while hoisting a two-foot-long rawhide bone almost bowled her over. "Cleo?" Belle called again.

A five-year-old girl in pink ballerina regalia glared imperiously down from the landing. "That's not Cleo," she announced while scrutinizing the guest and adopting a pose that resembled a lilliputian Elizabeth Regina. "I know you. You're Uncle Rosco's fiancée." The word was pronounced *fancy* and contained all the iciness a five-year-old can project when dealing with a beloved uncle's future bride.

"Hi, Effie." Belle pasted on what she hoped was an engaging smile while another, larger dog careened around the corner followed by the girl's older brother. He, in turn, was pursued by three additional eight-year-olds armed to the teeth with purple and silver intergalactic-style guns that shot rays of red light while emitting teeth-tingling squeals. "Where's Mom?" the ballerina shouted. "Uncle Rosco's *fancy's* here."

"Mom!" the boy bellowed as he and his friends pelted out the door Belle had left ajar.

"I like your costume, Effie," Belle said, but her miniature nemesis only increased her scowl. Uncle Rosco had always been Effie's favorite; his *fancy* was an interloper of the highest order. "It's not a costume; it's an *outfit*. That's what Mommy calls it." Then Effie vanished up the stairs.

Belle took a breath and walked the length of the living room. "Cleo? Hello?"

The masonry saw stopped whining. "She's out in the garage arguing with Geoffrey about the color of the cabinets." Sharon poked her head through the interior window that joined the upper kitchen and family area to the lower living room. "Cleo says it's too red or something, but Geoff is sticking to his guns. I guess we're into homeowner meltdown." Sharon grinned with her Vermonter's fleeting sense of joy. A well-padded six foot one with arms and hands that could easily handle the stone and marble that earned her her daily bread, she had a big face; and her dark hair was cropped so short it bristled over her broad and unperturbed brow. Sharon reminded Belle of a friendly giant peering down from the window. "What's up?"

"I just stopped by to see how things were progressing—"

Sharon's head disappeared. Belle heard slabs of marble being repositioned while a voice boomed above the noise. "Not to worry. We'll get it done in time, Belle. You got bride jitters, is all. I've worked with Geoff long enough to know he always delivers."

Alone in the living room, Belle's "I'm not nervous in the least," was drowned by another screech of the masonry saw. White marble powder billowed through the open window. She walked outside, clutched her jacket against the morning chill, and entered the garage.

"*Cherry* is what I wanted, Geoffrey. That looks like *magenta*." The word was elongated into an operatic sigh; the eldest of the Polycrates siblings, Cleo had always had the temperament of a Greek diva. She turned around as her future sister-in-law entered. "*Belle. Honeybunch.* Come give me *your* opinion. Doesn't this color seem overly pink? I mean, an entire *wall* of this shade . . . ?" She let the words trail off as she and Geoff Wright returned their concentration to the cabinetry in question. The entire garage was filled with similar cuts of wood in various stages of completion.

"I want *authenticity*," Cleo insisted. "I don't want *plasticized* American *kitsch*. That's why I hired you. You're an *artist*. Everyone told me you were the *best*. . . . Went to that fancy *design* school in Rhode Island and everything . . . I want the kitchen cabinets *hand-crafted*, and I want them to *look* hand-crafted."

Belle studied the doors and drawers strewn about the garage. Eight days until the wedding, eight days before forty or fifty guests were to descend upon Cleo's house for a postnuptial party, and the "new" kitchen was still inoperable. *Forget the platters of homemade goodies,* Belle told herself, *we'll be lucky if there's enough space for take-out pizza boxes.*

"It's cherry, Cleo," Geoffrey insisted. "Just like you asked me for. . . . Now, I could apply more burnt umber if you'd like, but you didn't want too much brown, remember?"

Cleo sighed pointedly.

"Let me try additional umber. . . . I think you'll like it." Geoff winked at Belle as if he'd just noticed her standing there and added a cheery "Hiya, Tinker Bell. You've done something new with your hair."

Belle stifled a wince. Why is it, she wondered, that certain people attract the most hideous nicknames? Born Annabella Graham, she'd been dubbed "A. Graham Belle" by waggish high-school classmates, then "AnnaGram" because of her career as an editor of crossword puzzles. Now Geoffrey Wright, wisecracking cabinetmaker, Ivy League graduate and enthusiastic resident of the Northern provinces had decided on "Tinker Bell," which Cleo, Cleo's sister Ariadne, and their respective husbands and children found excruciatingly funny. The only member of the extended Polycrates clan who didn't crack a smile was the family matriarch, Helen.

"I thought I'd try a new style for the wedding." Belle patted her lacquered and upswept blond hair with inexperienced hands. "With only *a week to go*, I didn't want to wait and leave experiments for the day before."

The hint about timing eluded the combatants. Cleo's focus remained on the cabinet door while Geoff affixed Belle with another bright grin. "If you're taking a poll, I like it better the way you always wear it. Don't mess it up with goo and shellac. Be 'authentic' like her highness says."

"If you're *certain* I won't *regret* this decision, Geoffrey . . ." Cleo's tone had turned simpering.

"White Barre marble and cherry wood. You can't get more New England, Cleo."

"See you both later," Belle said, although no one responded.

She walked back into the May sunlight and her blessedly empty car. After driving several blocks through the suburban subdivision, she turned into a side street and switched off the ignition. *Rosco warned me,* she told herself; *it's a big family . . . and a Greek family. There are uncles and aunts, nieces and nephews, and each of those people has many friends, colleagues, neighbors, enemies, and rivals. What does an only child raised by two absentminded Anglophile professors know about communal living?*

She stared through the windshield. The clouds were rapidly darkening and the wind beginning to gust. All the same, a group of robins bounced among the branches of a nearby apple tree, their breasts fat and red against the burgeoning greenery. If she rolled down the window or released the door handle, Belle knew she would hear them calling boldly to one another. Open: the noise of life. Closed: the silence of solitude. *Open and shut,* she thought. *Life should be so easy. Or as Rayanne might put it: Open, hopin', copin'.*

CHAPTER

4

The Marriage License Bureau lay within the City Hall complex fronting Winthrop Drive. The tall central building had been constructed of granite, now aged to a rough gray white by one hundred fifty years of Massachusetts winters. Doric columns surmounted spacious steps that led from street level to the showy entry. It was a place that exuded power, responsibility, the wisdom of long-dead town fathers, and the austerity of their verdicts. As she circled the building looking for a parking place, Belle glanced up at the frieze carved within the pediment: sailing ships tossed on a turbulent sea. Newcastle had once been a whaling city; the ocean had made her rich; benign or perilous weather was another form of judgment.

She circled City Hall three times, finally snagging a parking spot on Third Street, and glanced at her watch. "Oh, geez . . . late again." Belle sighed. Why was it, she wondered, that she had such difficulty maintaining a schedule? Was it genetic, like her inability to gauge north from south and east from west, or tell a joke without garbling the punch line?

She locked her car, hurried down Winthrop Drive, pelted up the exterior granite steps, and dashed toward the interior marble stairway. On the third floor, the central rotunda revealed a series of narrow corridors that glimmered uneasily with fluorescent light. *Marriage Licenses*, Belle read. She rounded the corner and ran.

"Rosco! Hi! Sorry! I was working with Rayanne, and then I stopped in at Cleo's. . . ." Breathless, she beamed at him. The world, all at once, seemed reliable and good. An open-and-shut case, she realized. Her smile grew; her gray eyes danced. "Geoff, the miracle man, is fussing with wood stains. Cleo is, well, you know . . ." She shook her head; a pin holding her carefully sculpted locks dropped onto the floor. "Oops! Maybe the fifties glamour-girl look is out."

"I love you the way you look every day . . . any day." Rosco grinned and moved closer, but the proximity of several nervous couples and a termagant clerk made him keep a decorous distance. "How were things at Sister Mary Catherine's?"

Belle's eyes suddenly narrowed. "I'm afraid there's a property battle brewing."

Rosco shook his head but didn't speak.

"Can't those people be left in peace, Rosco? If anyone's responsible for cleaning up that section of town, it's the nuns and Father Tom. And now their hard work is being thrown in their faces . . . rumors that the shelters are attracting addicts and criminals; it's stupid. They're the ones who pushed out the druggies in the first place."

"Anywhere but my backyard . . . That's progress for you," Rosco muttered.

"Progress, my eye. It's plain, old-fashioned greed!"

Belle's vehement righteousness brought another smile to Rosco's face. "And how was the rest of your morning? Everything in the burbs okay?"

Belle let out a worried sigh. "The kitchen's never going to be finished in time." She paused, searching for a tactful approach. "Do you think Cleo would mind terribly if we moved the party? My house might be able to accommodate—"

"Yes, I *do* think Cleo would mind. Forget *think*; I *know* she'd mind. She wants to welcome you into the family." Rosco watched Belle's mouth grow thin and tight. "She's my sister. She and Ariadne; my brother, Danny; my mom . . ." Rosco counted the four of them off on his fingers. "But they're not me, Belle. We don't have to spend more time with the Polycrates clan than you're comfortable with."

"What about your 'Third Tuesday Family Shoot-Outs'?"

"And we don't have to go to that every month, either. Besides, you said you enjoyed them."

Bewilderment creased Belle's brow. "I did! I do! It's just that—"

"We're not going to be swallowed whole. We'll have our own life, I promise."

Belle stared at the floor. "You wore socks!" she said with a sudden grin.

"Yeah . . . well . . . in honor of the big occasion."

"You don't have to change, Rosco. Just because we're getting married."

"There. See? You don't change, I don't change, and everyone lives happily ever after."

* * *

The clerk looked like a stick figure drawn in pencil; her skin, hair, even the clothes that covered her slight frame were colorless and flat. She even had a tentative way of moving, darting her fingers across the government forms, weighing official stamps and ballpoint pens as if she were about to drop them and run for the hills while her smile—such as it was—looked as if it had been added as an afterthought by someone unaware that lips should curve upward in pleasure. When the woman spoke, however, she was transformed. The clerk had the voice of a tiger. "Name?"

"Rosco Polycrates. I wrote it on line—" He tried to point through the glass separating license applicants from those in power.

R-O-S-C-O-*E* she penned in dark block letters.

"There is no *e* on the end," he said. "My folks—"

The woman interrupted with an impatient sigh, then unsuccessfully attempted to erase the additional letter.

"Age?"

"Thirty-eight. It says so right—"

"Sir. My job is to verify pertinent data. Yours is to supply it. Sex?"

"Why not? That's one of the reasons we're getting married, isn't it?"

If looks could kill, the clerk would have turned Rosco to dust.

Rosco backtracked. "I guess we should list that as male." Belle rolled her eyes and squeezed his hand. "I'm a private investigator," he added as if the information would confirm the accuracy of his statements. "Formerly with the police department."

The clerk glared. "Your past employment is of no consequence here, sir. Nor does it impress me. Marital status?"

"Where did it say that? I guess I missed that question. . . . Why else would I be here?"

The woman's piercing stare only intensified.

"Divorced, I guess. Married once before. It didn't work out. I was too young."

The official pen paused above the smudged form. "Sir. Are you or are you not free to apply for a marriage license?"

"Free . . . absolutely."

The clerk's basilisk mask dispensed with Rosco. "You'll have to redo this form, sir. The errors make it quite illegible. It will never reproduce clearly on our copy machine." She turned her attention to Belle. "Name?" she demanded before proceeding through an identical litany.

"Thirty-three . . . female . . . also divorced."

"I know you!" the clerk suddenly announced. "You're the crossword editor at the *Evening Crier*! The one who solved those crimes!"

"Actually, we both—" Belle began, but Rosco tugged on her hand.

"I read about you in *Personality* magazine. You're prettier than your picture. I would have assumed *Personality* hired professional makeup artists and stylists."

"No, they—" Belle started to respond, but the clerk interrupted with an abrupt "What's it like to catch a murderer?"

"I didn't actually catch—"

"*Solved the crime,*" the clerk interjected. "That's what the article said. It's the same thing. I have a near-photographic memory. I can quote everything I've read in *Per-*

sonality. The picture was in your home office, with all that black and white crossword decor. The interviewer said you prefer working at home to being at the *Crier*. 'The Queen of Cryptics,' that was the title of the story." She added an airy: "I don't do those puzzles myself. I hate writing in pencil. You see what a mess your fiancé made of his form when it needed to be corrected."

Belle attempted a warm smile. "You could try using a pen. That's what I do—"

"You can't erase a pen at all."

Belle opened her mouth to speak, but another gentle squeeze from Rosco's fingers silenced her.

"Individual conducting the ceremony?" This time, the question was directed at Rosco.

"Oh, we're getting married on a boat," Belle interjected. "Senator Hal Crane's private yacht. It was his nephew who—"

But the clerk had already dispensed with the famous Queen of Cryptics. "In whose waters will you be getting married, sir?" Her voice had an ominous ring.

Rosco cleared his throat. He stepped closer to the Plexiglas window. "Whose waters?"

"If you're married at sea, you may—or you may not— be in Newcastle waters, and thus within—or *not within*— the jurisdiction of our municipality."

"What happens if we're not?" Belle ignored Rosco's furtive warning.

"Then this department cannot help you." The clerk moved her glance to the line of couples waiting near the door. "Next?"

"But—" Belle began.

"Please secure the coordinates from the vessel's captain. If he—or she—plans to cruise within Newcastle's maritime domain, this Bureau of Marriage Licenses will be happy to assist you. Otherwise, you'll need to apply to the township appropriate to your position—"

Belle opened her mouth. Her face was pink, and the scalp beneath her pale blond hair rosy with anger. "We're being married by the captain!"

"Is he—or she—a certified justice of the peace? That's another issue you'll need to clarify. If he—or she—fails to hold the proper credentials . . . Well, certainly there would be a legitimate contention of legality. The celebrant, and in your case I seem to be using the term very loosely, must endorse this license. He—or she—must hold the proper credentials."

Belle started to reply. Rosco stopped her.

"We'll be back this afternoon," he said.

"It's Friday, sir," was her triumphant answer. "We have limited afternoon hours."

"We'll be back," Rosco repeated.

It was in the rotunda that they found Lever. Al and Rosco had been partners back in the days when Rosco was with the NPD. The two had always been oil and water, frost and steam, day and night. They were also true and long-time friends, and Al considered that the forthcoming nuptials were due to his direct aid, advice and intervention. Lever was to be Rosco's best man; it was a position he approached with more than a little awe.

"Hey, Polly—crates. Belle. I was just coming to see how you two lovebirds were faring with Miss Gestapo in there." Reflexively, he reached for his cigarettes, then pulled his hand away. "I forgot. City Hall. Another famous smokeless zone. Shows you what lengths a friend will go to in the line of nuptial duties." He coughed, wheezed, then glowered at the staircase. "I read somewhere that climbing steps is great exercise. It's aerobic, or something."

"Any exercise is better than none, Al."

"I play golf, Polly—crates, in case your feeble brain forgot." Another wheezing fit attacked Lever. He pretended to ignore the bemused glance that passed between his former partner and Belle. "Three flights of stairs aren't exercise; they're hell." He regretfully patted the cigarette packet again. "Hey, you two aren't looking so hot. Don't tell me your license was denied? There wasn't a road test, was there?"

Rosco answered, "A long story, Al. Something about ship coordinates."

Lever looked horrified. "You're not going to postpone the wedding, are you?"

"Not if we can help it," Belle said as the three began descending the stairs. "We just need to talk to the captain." Then she changed the subject; she'd become truly fond of the irascible Lever. "You're not looking very chipper either, Al."

"A vagrant turned up dead this morning. Smashed skull. No cash. Dog food cans in his pockets. What's the world coming to when people have to eat stuff like that?"

Belle's bright face darkened. "One of the residents of the Saint Augustine Mission?"

"No one seemed to be missing. But that doesn't mean he never passed through there."

Belle's expression remained troubled. She didn't speak for a long minute, but Rosco knew her mind was whirling with possibilities. "And someone killed him? Why?"

"No telling. Fight over a bottle, robbery, bad debt. It might take a while, but we'll figure it out."

"Did anyone know him?" Belle continued. "Was he from around here?"

"Carlyle IDed the body twenty minutes ago. Local guy name of Carson."

"Not *Freddie* Carson?" Rosco asked.

"That's right, Frederick Carson. You know him?"

"Sort of. He had cans of dog food on him?"

"Hey, Polly—crates, you better get over these wedding bell woes and concentrate. Yes, dog food."

"I used to see Freddie Carson around town," Rosco said slowly. "I helped him out once or twice; bought him a cup of coffee, a sandwich. He wasn't eating dog food, Al, he had a dog. A puppy. He'd found a puppy."

"What kind of puppy?"

"A mutt. No tail. Kind of scruffy. About yea big." Rosco raised his hands and held his palms eight inches apart.

"Well, there wasn't any scruffy puppy there when we came across him."

CHAPTER

5

Belle remained silent as she climbed into Rosco's aging Jeep. He closed the door behind her, walked around the car, and sat in the driver's seat. "Are you okay?"

She looked through the passenger-side window, her face pinched and sad. "Why would someone murder a homeless person, Rosco?"

"What Al said, I guess. A fight over a liquor bottle . . . an unpaid debt—"

"What if something more sinister is involved?"

"Such as?"

"I don't know yet . . . I just feel there's a missing element. Maybe something to do with discrediting the homeless shelters."

"Al's a good cop, Belle. If there's a connection to this gossip about the Peterman brothers, he'll uncover it."

Belle nodded thoughtfully but didn't speak as Rosco eased into the steady stream of traffic clogging Winthrop Drive. "Where did you leave your car?"

"What? Oh . . . down on Third, I think. Or maybe Fourth. But it was a good spot. No meter. I should be fine all day. . . . Oh, look at that. A newspaper vending machine's been knocked into the street. It's a *Crier* box, too." She picked up Rosco's car phone, punched in the *Crier*'s central number, reported the problem, then replaced the receiver. "I don't know why kids think its such a blast to vandalize these kiosks."

"Money?" Rosco offered as he drove. "Maybe we should pick up your car and drive over to the yacht separately. Traffic will be worse later on. You're sure you're not in one of those areas that's only good until four P.M.?"

"My parking spot is fine, Rosco, really. I'm not in a tow zone."

"On Third or Fourth Street? That sounds unlikely."

"I can show you the exact spot if you want. I pulled in right behind a big green thing. It had enormous wheels."

Rosco chuckled. "What if the big green thing moves? How will you find your car then?"

Belle let out her own small laugh. "Okay, Mr. Perfect Driving Record. And I do emphasize *record*. It's only perfect because you never get caught; and when you do get caught, you give them the mystical ex-cop handshake, and they let you go. At least I stop and ask for directions. When I get lost, I know it . . . and am willing to admit it." She glanced through the passenger-side window again. "Another vandalized vending machine. What's going on here?" She picked up the phone, reported the second situation, then returned to her pensive state. "I hope whoever killed Carson didn't hurt that puppy."

Rosco looked at her. "The person did more than hurt its owner."

Belle didn't respond for a long, disturbed minute.

"You're right. Freddie probably had insurmountable problems . . . and I'm worrying about his dog!"

"Carson was an okay guy. A little flaky, but that's to be expected given a street person's history . . . and diet."

"And here I am, fussing over a pet!"

They drove on in silence through weather that had turned ominous. Black-streaked clouds scudded across a lowering sky; the ocean breeze smelled dank, and the budding blossoms of pears and chestnuts huddling beside the brick and granite of the old town center seemed to retire into themselves as if winter still tarried in the air.

"Let's hope our wedding day isn't like this," Belle finally said. "What happened to May flowers?"

"Let's hope Buzzards Bay is calm," Rosco answered. "A ceremony in which the groom turns green and pants like a dying fish doesn't sound appealing." He exited Nathaniel Hawthorne Street and turned left onto Harbor Road.

Belle nestled close. "You're a prince to do this for me. . . . Married at sea! Plus, I have a theory: This entire experience is going to exorcise your seasickness forever."

"We have to secure the license first, Belle."

She smiled. "Let's not forget the certified justice of the peace." Belle leaned against him, and he draped an arm across her shoulder.

At the guardhouse of the Patriot Yacht Club marina, they were directed to Senator Crane's berth and the magnificent motor yacht *Akbar*. Tied to a gray brown pier among the choppy waves of a steel-colored sea, the yacht still managed to glitter. Seventy feet of teak and mahogany, fresh white paint, spar varnish the color of liquid butterscotch, and brass so gleaming its reflection could harm the eye, the *Akbar* exuded that indefinable aura known as class. Built for the senator's father in the 1930s, the yacht had long been a familiar sight in the many playgrounds of the very rich.

Despite his status as dyed-in-the-wool landlubber, Rosco let out an appreciative whistle as they approached. "I guess if we're going to get married on a boat, this is the one to use."

"I love you," Belle answered. Then her face fell. "Sara's here."

"How do you know?"

"Her car."

"Is it a big green thing?"

"Very amusing." Belle nodded toward the reserved parking. Sure enough, there was Sara Crane Briephs's 1956 Cadillac. Highly polished chrome, black paint so densely waxed it had beaded with water, the vehicle was as recognizable and redoubtable as its singular owner, the senator's octogenarian older sister. "I thought we were going to have a little time alone," Belle murmured.

"Maybe that part doesn't come until after the wedding."

Belle's mouth remained tense.

"Dear ones!" The lady herself stepped from the yacht's gangway. "Darling Albert informed me you were on your way down here. Some problem with the license . . . naval coordinates or some such nonsense! Belle, dear! You're looking awfully bereft for a bride-to-be."

Belle curved her lips into a semblance of pleasure. She genuinely liked and admired Sara and normally greatly enjoyed her company. Today, however, Belle felt a strong impulse to call, *Time out! Rosco and I are getting married, and we could use less input from our friends and family.*

Instead, she gave Sara an affectionate embrace and was rewarded with a doting smile. Belle noted the tidy suit and silk scarf, the white cotton gloves, the navy blue pumps: Newcastle's grande dame was dressed for an important excursion. The only thing she lacked was a wide-brimmed hat, but perhaps she'd deemed the weather too inclement for elegant headgear. "Albert was coughing horribly when I spoke with him. We must persuade him to stop smoking. It's taking a toll on his health. You talk to him, Rosco. He's your best man, after all."

Above Sara's perfectly coiffed white head, Rosco winked at Belle. "*Albert* is his own boss."

"He has a wife, dear boy. What does she say about all this? No *man* is his own master, Rosco. You're about to be married. You should know that by now." Sara returned to Belle. "Now, dear heart, I'll handle everything. Captain Lancia is desperately willing to help. He's the *Akbar*'s new chief. Where my brother found him, I haven't a clue. But from the man's Mastroianni eyes and basso voice, I'd guess Naples. There's such marvelous mystery to that port. . . . At any rate, he and I will organize all details for the cruise: which waters, and under which municipality's jurisdiction, and all that other folderol—"

"But—" Belle began.

"And if need be, I'll accompany you to City Hall myself and inform that little snip of a clerk exactly what happens to government employees who overreach themselves."

"I don't believe—" Rosco tried to interject, but Sara bulldozed past him.

"After all, my brother has been overspending taxpayers' money for a good many years. . . ."

Belle sighed inwardly. How were these various folks going to coexist on her wedding day? A boisterous family of Greek-Americans, doughty Sara with her dated opinions about noblesse oblige, and Belle's own father, who'd become markedly incommunicative when she'd written to inform him that she was engaged to a private detective, one who'd attended a *state* university, to boot.

"There was a homicide downtown this morning," Rosco said in an attempt to curtail Sara's monologue. "In Adams Alley. A homeless man."

The old lady stopped in her tracks. "Why . . . ? Why would someone do that? Isn't it cruel enough that people are forced to live on the streets?" Sara paused for a moment, then seemed to take a greater interest. "And Adams Alley? Very interesting that it should happen right in the middle of our new empowerment zone."

"Pardon me?"

"Please Rosco, don't assume I'm a naive old bat. We all know what's going on in that area of the city and who the power brokers are. Tax incentives to encourage neighborhood growth, my foot. The only growth I can see shows up in the landlords' pocketbooks. And we all know who sits on the top of that heap."

"I wouldn't want to jump to any conclusion, Sara. This death may be as simple as a squabble over a liquor bottle."

"If I've learned anything in my eighty-some years, it's that life is not *simple*."

"He had a dog," Belle added, "a puppy—"

Beneath her powder and hint of rouge, the staunch old face blanched. "Don't tell me the dog was killed, too!" A hint of tears appeared in Sara's ice-blue eyes.

Rosco answered. He tried to sound reasonable and calming. "The puppy disappeared, Sara. Just probably ran off."

"We'll have to find it, then."

Rosco affixed his professional smile. "At the moment, Belle and I have more pressing business. I'm sure the dog will turn up—"

Sara's imperious voice cut in. "Your fiancée and I will attend to the details of your marriage license. You, Rosco, will find that poor, defenseless dog. It's the least we can do."

"I appreciate your concern, Sara, but let's let Lever and his homicide boys have a—"

But Sara Crane Briephs refused to be superseded. "You misunderstand me, Rosco. I'm engaging you professionally. I want that dog found."

"Kit. That's what Freddie Carson named her. You know, like Kit Carson, the scout in the Western territories . . . ? Her fur was a little mangy like one of those coonskin caps you see in secondhand shops, and she didn't have a tail, but she was a cute little pup."

Rosco dragged a discarded plastic milk crate over to the man's side and sat. In an almost Pavlovian response, he said, "What do you mean by *was?*"

"I dunno, I guess now that Freddie's a *was,* I assume the dog's a *was* too. A puppy doesn't survive long on its own. . . . I had a dog once. . . . You don't have any smokes on you, by any chance?"

Rosco shook his head and looked the man over a second time. Determining his age was almost impossible. He could have been thirty-six or sixty-three. He hadn't shaved or bathed in a week, and he reeked of alcohol. Rosco had found him sitting at the end of the abandoned Seventh Street pier; feet dangling over the edge, an empty pint of cheap rosé wine lying beside him on the weatherbeaten wood planks. Rosco had discovered his name was Gus, and depending on whether he was on or off the wagon, his home was the Saint Augustine Mission or the streets of Newcastle or Boston. Presently, it was the streets of Newcastle.

"Did you know that Kit Carson was breveted a brigadier-general of volunteers after the Civil War?" Gus provided this curious bit of information as he spat into the water below. Evening had set in; the storm clouds had lifted, and the lights across the Newcastle River made the scene oddly romantic, considering the conversation and the principals involved.

"You got me there, Gus. I don't know much about Kit Carson."

"Christopher, his given name was. Breveted March of 1865. For gallantry in the Battle of Valverde," Gus slurred. He raised a finger for emphasis. "It's interesting, because the battle was actually in February of '62. Things moved slower back then. Course Kit died three years later. . . . Too little, too late. That's how I look at it. Just another case of the government makin' someone's life miserable. Custer, there's another one who was promoted to brigadier-general of volunteers. In 1863, two years after he graduated from West Point. His younger brother died with him at Little Big Horn. A lot of people aren't aware of that. They don't realize—"

Rosco interrupted the rambling tale. "How long did you know Freddie?"

"Say, you don't have a couple of bucks you can spare, do you? I was thinking a taste of wine might be pleasant about now. Warm me up. This hasn't been the mildest of Mays. You're welcome to join me. A regular little cocktail party." Gus chuckled to himself.

"I'm not going to lecture you, Gus. But what I will do is drive you to Father Tom's mission. You need to get yourself cleaned up."

"I'm not ready to see him or Heartbreak Hotel again. I don't need that kind of pressure."

"Your decision. The mission is a whole lot warmer and drier than the streets." Rosco was silent a moment. He thought about Gus, and the murdered Freddie, Kit Carson, George Armstrong Custer, lives misspent and lives fulfilled. "Find the dog," Sara had said. How could anyone search for a lost animal and ignore a human being? "When was the last time you saw Freddie?"

"You're contendin' you're not a cop, right?"

"Does it make a difference?"

"Yeah, it makes a difference. I got no use for cops. I got no use for the government."

"Right. Unless, of course, there's some crazy out there who's decided it's time to start killing off street people. You'll have plenty of use for cops then, I would imagine."

Gus didn't respond. Rosco let the prediction sink in before he spoke again. "As I said, a lady asked me to look for his dog. I didn't really know Freddie—I bought him a cup of coffee once in a while—but that was my only contact. He seemed like a nice enough guy. . . . Did he have a regular place to hang out? Somewhere he might have deposited Kit? An abandoned building? One of the old train sheds?"

"You got me."

Rosco paused, then tried another tack. "Okay, let's return to this question: When was the last time you saw Freddie?"

"Alive?"

Rosco studied Gus for a moment. "You mean you saw him dead? You were in Adams Alley last night?"

"I don't know. You got me confused. Maybe I walked down there last night. Maybe it was the night before . . . or a week ago. I don't know. Maybe Freddie was sleepin'; maybe he was dead. I don't know, pal. I been drinkin' straight for seven days. I don't remember anything."

"So, when you saw Freddie . . . Kit wasn't with him. Is that correct?"

Gus raised his voice to a shout. "I'm tellin' ya I don't know. Maybe the pup was sleeping alongside him, maybe not. It's dark in that alley. . . . Wait a minute. Are you sayin' I killed Freddie? Is that it?"

"Relax, Gus."

"Don't 'relax' me, buster."

"Look, Gus. I'm going to the mission to talk with Father Tom. Why don't you come with me? I'll give you a lift. Get yourself a meal and a bed . . . At least for tonight."

"I don't want to see Father Tom."

Gus raised his wine bottle, held it to the light, and confirmed its empty status. He tossed it into the inky water. "Why don't you leave me alone," he grumbled. "I take back my offer to have you join me for a drink. I *rescind* the invitation."

"Have it your own way." Rosco stood and walked down the pier to his Jeep leaving Gus alone with his demons.

Father Thomas Witwicki looked more like a mobster than a man of the cloth. Midfifties, six feet five, and close to three hundred pounds, he had a nose that had been broken three times, short-cropped fiery red hair, and a limp that everyone assumed had come from a kneecapping in an earlier life. He'd founded the Saint Augustine Mission fifteen years prior with the sole resources of his own muscle and brawn and the sometimes capricious efforts of the very men he'd felt called to save.

Like the two nuns who supervised the nearby women's shelter, the priest had done his share of cerebral and spiritual arm-twisting to inspire a local business consortium to provide two vacant commercial buildings, which had been transformed into second-floor dormitories and two street-level recreation areas and dining halls that fed any and all who were hungry, providing they were clean and sober. Although he seldom wore his clerical collar, he was such a presence in Newcastle, no one ever mistook him for anyone other than who he was: good old Father Tom.

When Rosco entered the Saint Augustine kitchen, he found the mission's founder wearing a white apron and kneading bread dough. The priest looked up. Strangers wandering in and out of the premises didn't perturb him in the least. "Wash your hands. There's an apron in that closet. . . . You can give me a hand. There's nothing better for your soul than making bread."

"Actually, I just wanted to ask you a few questions."

"That much is obvious. You're either a reporter or a police officer, and you want answers about Freddie Carson. Well, you're going to have to work for them. Grab an apron, or grab that doorknob and go back where you came from."

Rosco did as he was told. With a white apron tied to his waist, he crossed to the stainless steel table where Father Tom was working.

"I have to be honest with you," Rosco said. "I'm not much of a cook."

"You don't have to be. You just need a little forearm muscle, which you seem to have. Better roll your sleeves up another fold or two. . . . Wash your hands and dip 'em into the flour. Then grab a handful of dough about *yea* big, knead it like this for a minute or two, form it into a loaf shape, and place it in one of those pans. . . . Got it? A local supermarket used to supply our bread . . . stuff that had passed the expiration date. But the loaves began showing up moldy, so now we make our own. The same goes for the women's shelter."

"We? Where's the *we?* I only see you."

"The *we* in this case is you and me, young man."

Rosco smiled, dipped his palms into the flour, and extended his right hand to Father Tom. "My name's Polycrates. Rosco Polycrates."

"Greek, are you?"

"Third generation."

"Thomas Witwicki. Don't ask me how it was spelled in Poland. The same as the poet, I would imagine. . . . Father Tom will do. So, what is it? Police or reporter?"

"I'm a private detective. I was with the Newcastle department at one time, but this visit's nothing official. I'm trying to locate Freddie Carson's dog, Kit."

"Don't yank at the dough. You're not hauling in fishing nets, Rosco. Knead it firmly, but slowly and evenly. Otherwise it won't rise. . . . I'm afraid I don't have information on the dog. But it seems odd that you'd be more concerned about the whereabouts of an animal than the fact that a man has lost his life."

"Maybe it's the Saint Francis in me. . . ."

Father Tom didn't crack even a tiny smile. "We take religion seriously here."

"So do I." Rosco's expression had turned equally grave. He kneaded dough for a moment. "I have a hunch that finding Carson's dog might possibly lead to the killer."

"How is that?"

"The dog's a missing piece of the picture."

"The pup could have run off."

"It could have." Rosco paused. "I spoke with a fella named Gus half an hour ago. You know him?"

"Gus? Of course. Where's he gotten to?"

"I found him sitting at the end of the old Seventh Street pier."

"Sober?"

"Not by a long shot."

Father Tom didn't speak for a minute. "Gus is in and out of the mission on a regular basis. Clean and sober; that's the rule. It's playing hardball, I know, but it's something these guys understand. Gus used to be a professor of American history. Did he tell you?"

"We didn't get past the nineteenth century. The conversation fizzled after George Armstrong Custer."

"Gus bounces back and forth between here and Boston. There are more shelters up there, and they aren't as tyrannical about alcohol as I am. I think Gus sees this as a kind of drying-out clinic. AA doesn't work for everyone."

"Was the same scenario true for Freddie?" Rosco presented his kneaded dough to Father Tom. "Is this okay?"

"Fine. Just drop it into a loaf pan. . . . No, Freddie never drank. He'd been at Saint Augustine's for almost three years. In fact, he was my main bread baker."

"The police found an empty bottle next to his body."

"I don't know about that. But it couldn't have been Freddie's. It must have belonged to someone else."

Rosco refloured his hands, formed another ball of dough, and began kneading it. "Then why was he sleeping on the streets? I mean, if he was clean and sober, he could've stayed here. Isn't that right?"

Father Tom leaned his large frame on the countertop behind him, folded his beefy arms across his chest, and let out a weighty sigh. "It was my fault. . . . The darn dog . . . Freddie found her on the street, a scrawny little mutt. No tail. That was about two weeks ago. Maybe a little more. He brought her here. . . ." His voice trailed off. "I had to make a tough decision. What I mean is, we can't permit animals to live on the property. We serve food. Freddie's work was in the kitchen. . . . Anyway, I told him he'd have to take the dog to the pound. . . ."

"And he wouldn't."

"He was afraid they'd put her to sleep. Which, I suppose they would have."

"I don't know, Father. Sure, the pup was scruffy looking, but I think someone would have adopted her."

"You saw Freddie's dog?"

"I bought him a cup of coffee last week. A couple of times in fact."

Silence lay between them. Rosco was the first to speak.

"So, your decision was that either the dog left, or Freddie would have to go."

Father Tom grabbed another ball of dough and punched it down. "Don't make it sound so black and white. We're dealing with the Board of Health here. Besides, some of our residents are allergic to dogs; some are scared to death of them. Yes, the puppy had to go. Freddie understood that. We can't bend the rules. It's not good for the men. . . . Did you see that empty warehouse across the street?"

"No."

"The building's been sold. One of those high-end food markets. Imported cheeses, flavored olive oil, caviar, the works. Two doors away there are plans for an antique shop, and there's talk of an art gallery in the old Tyler fish packing building." Father Tom's tone had turned unexpectedly steely. "The neighborhood's changing. It's becoming trendy to live in this part of the city, and the mission's under a good deal of pressure from real estate interests. If I harbored a dog, the Peterman brothers would make certain we were shut down quicker than you can say Jiminy Cricket."

"How well do you know Gus?"

"Only what I shared with you. He wanders back and forth to Boston. Used to be a professor. Dartmouth, I believe."

"Where'd you get that information?"

"Everything comes from the men themselves. They can lie to me, of course, but what's the point? If they have veterans' benefits, social security, disability, pension, et cetera, I try to contact the appropriate agency and help them get back on their feet. If the stories don't wash, they're only cheating themselves."

Rosco finished sculpting another ball of dough; he wiped his hands on the front of his apron. "How many of these loaf pans do you need to fill tonight?"

"All of them."

"How long will that take?"

"With you here, no more than an hour. Would you like a cup of coffee or tea while you work?"

Rosco shook his head. "Thanks for the offer, though." He thought for a minute. "Do you know Gus's last name?"

"Taylor. Why? Do you think he might have killed Freddie?"

"I'm only looking for a lost dog, remember?"

CHAPTER

7

Ten o'clock Saturday morning was an unlikely time for a jewelry heist. History had taught Rosco that the average crook liked to sleep well past noon on the weekends. So when the phenomenally shrill burglar alarm at Hudson's Diamond Exchange sounded, he was as startled as the other customers and the several employees. Out of reflex, he reached for his pistol, a .32 caliber semiautomatic he seldom carried. The only thing he found under his jacket was a nicely tooled leather belt, a birthday gift from Belle.

At the sound of the siren's blare, the sales manager scooped Rosco's wedding bands from a gray velvet pad on the glass countertop, returned the rings to the showcase, locked it, and dropped the keys into a sealed steel box. The motion was so swift and agile Rosco believed he was watching a sleight-of-hand artist. The sales manager then addressed his attention to the front door and the individual who had instigated the disturbance.

"Sir, the police have been summoned by an automatic alarm system; all activity in the shop is being monitored by video cameras. It would be in your best interest to move slowly and calmly. In fact, you may care to leave before the police arrive."

It was Al Lever to whom these words were directed.

Lever's gaze took in the customers' horrified faces before his glance came to rest on Hudson's manager. "I am the police, fella," he said. He pulled his gold detective's badge from his jacket and held it in the air for all to see. Audible sighs emanated from everyone except Rosco, who was laughing. Al glowered at him.

"Well, *officer,*" the head clerk simpered, "your gun must have set off our metal detectors. You are carrying a weapon, I presume?"

Lever only nodded. He returned the badge to the breast pocket of his navy blue windbreaker.

"And how long will you be with us today, sir? I wouldn't want you to reactivate the alarm on your way out." The manager had become meekness itself. It was never wise to antagonize a law-enforcement officer . . . or a potential customer.

"Ten minutes, max."

The head clerk retreated through a rear doorway to reset the alarm while Rosco pointed to the street. "We've got company, Al."

Outside, a black and white patrol car came to a screeching halt, blue gray smoke drifting up from its fat tires. Two uniformed policemen jumped from the vehicle and positioned themselves behind a parked car, guns drawn.

"Arrgh," Lever moaned, "I'll go talk to them. A day off. Is it too much to ask? One simple day of blending in like any other civilian?"

Rosco thought it better not to mention that a poplin windbreaker combined with blue chinos, spit-polished brown Oxfords, and a cropped hairstyle didn't make for a blend-in appearance any more than a baseball cap imprinted with DEA or a rain jacket that spelled FBI. Instead, he said, "I appreciate your forsaking your day of leisure, Al."

"For you, Polly—crates . . ." Lever chugged outside and spoke to the cops.

A few minutes later, everything had returned to normal at Hudson's Diamond Exchange, and the wedding bands had been retrieved from the locked case.

"How do they get that writing inside there?" Lever asked as he inspected the engraving of Rosco and Belle's initials and their pending wedding date on the interior of the larger of the two bands.

"Hudson's has the best engraver in town," Rosco replied.

The manager signaled agreement with a smug smile while Lever replaced the rings on the gray velvet pad. His hand trembled.

"Are you all right, Al?"

"Look, Rosco, I'm not sure about all this. Why don't you hang onto the rings. The wedding's a week away. I'm going to lose them. I know it."

"Have you ever lost your badge?"

Lever shook his head.

"Your car keys? House keys? Credit cards? Your service revolver?"

Lever shrugged his shoulders, but his expression remained stubborn.

"Come on, Al, You're the best man. The rings are your responsibility. It's the only thing you have to do."

"I know, but I'm getting very nervous about this."

"You . . . ? You're getting nervous? I'm the one who's getting married. You don't see my hands shaking . . . yet."

"Yeah, but look who you're marrying. How could you go wrong with Belle? I'm just scared to death I'm going to lose the rings somehow." He added quietly, "She'd kill me if I did. You know she would."

"You're not going to lose them. Just put them in a safe place. Let your wife hold onto them—"

"Now, there's a less-than-brilliant notion. She loses her car keys on a monthly basis." At that moment, Lever's pager sounded with an annoying beep that once again attracted the attention of everyone in the store. He reached to his hip, shut off the noise, and glanced at the phone number displayed on the LED readout.

"I can't get a moment's peace." Lever looked at the sales manager. "Can I use your phone?"

"Certainly, *Officer.*"

The clerk produced a cordless telephone. Lever punched in the number without referring back to the pager; clearly it was a number he recognized. "Duty calls," he muttered to Rosco, then paced the floor for two or three minutes, all the while issuing inaudible orders to the person on the other end of the phone.

Rosco, along with everyone else in the store, watched the performance in silence. Finished, Lever disengaged the line and returned the phone to the sales clerk.

"Problems?" Rosco asked.

"You might say that. Another homeless person showed up dead. The bus depot, this time."

Rosco took a beat to digest the news. "It wasn't Gus Taylor, was it?"

"Who's Gus Taylor?"

"A sometime resident of the Saint Augustine Mission. I spoke with him last night. I was looking for Carson's dog."

"What?"

"It was Sara Briephs's idea."

Lever regarded his friend. "You and me need to talk, Polly—crates. What say we drive over to the scene together? And no, the body isn't Gus's. This time we've got a dead woman."

The two men exited the jewelry store, leaving the wedding bands resting peacefully atop the display case.

B elle looked at her watch, the third time in as many minutes. *Twenty to eleven,* she thought; *Rosco should have been here by now.* She gazed out the windows of her home office and thrust her hands deep into the pockets of her ribbed green cardigan, an ancient favorite that normally seemed as comforting as a bowl of chicken noodle soup. A steady drizzle had begun to fall. Unconsciously, she buttoned the cardigan, then unbuttoned it again; finally, she stuffed her hands back into her pockets. *Ten-forty, Saturday morning,* she thought. Rosco and Al must have finished picking up the wedding bands by now.

Her eyes moved from her own garden into the neighbors' tidy yard, her glance encompassing their meticulously restored and renovated home, the fanlight over the door, the flower boxes decoratively placed beneath each eighteenth-century window. Today, the ordinarily pleasant property looked neither cheering nor warm. *That poor, lost dog,* she thought. How can it stay dry in weather like this? What will it find to eat?

She shivered in empathy and left the window, looking at her watch for the fourth time as she wandered into the living room with its eclectic hodgepodge of thrift shop finds, then into the kitchen with its outmoded appliances, which Belle considered "charming" because she couldn't cook. Her feet never stopped moving; soon she was back in the living room, where she repositioned her newest acquisition, a large and squashy armchair covered in a 1950s cabbage rose print. She examined her watch again. The hour had advanced exactly five minutes.

Lawson's, she suddenly thought. *Perhaps Rosco went to Lawson's coffee shop expecting to meet me there. Perhaps we had our signals crossed.*

She charged back into the kitchen, grabbed the phone book, running her fingers down the pages until she found the listing for Newcastle's famous relic from the era of pink Formica luncheonettes.

"Yup?" she heard at the other end of the phone. Lawson's was not an eatery that stood on ceremony.

"Martha?" This was the self-styled head waitress. Martha had a yellow beehive hairdo and serious undergarments that crackled when she moved. "It's Belle. By any chance is—?"

"Haven't seen him, hon. I wondered when you two lovebirds were going to show up." Martha knew everyone in town, what hour they dined at her establishment, as well as what they habitually ate. "Two orders of bacon," she yelled to the unseen fry cook. "Extra crispy."

"Will you tell him I—?"

"Sure thing." The waitress pulled away the phone to talk to a customer. Belle heard the plinking sound of the cash register opening and then the drawer banging shut with metallic certainty. "Grooms get jitters. Give him some space, hon." The phone went dead before Belle had a chance to ask Martha what she meant.

Belle left the kitchen, reflexively rearranging the new chair's position as she passed. *Give him space,* she thought. *Is Martha insinuating that I'm crowding Rosco? Am I?*

She twisted the chair into another angle and returned to her office. *I can work,* she assured herself. *I can begin constructing a new crossword puzzle for the* Crier. *There's no point in wasting time stewing over casual remarks.* But this reasoning was specious, as Belle knew; Martha kept her ear to the ground. Despite Newcastle's size, very little happened in the city the waitress wasn't apprised of.

"Give him space," Belle repeated; then her thoughts shifted focus. Belle's brain was never still for long. "Space," she jotted on a scrap of paper, "time, capacity, opportunity, distance. Musical reference," she added, "aviation." The theme for a new cryptic had begun playing through her mind. "*Lost in———,*" she wrote. "*Out of——* *—out of time;*" beside this entry, she scribbled "*Edgar Allan Poe.*"

The phone rang. She peered at her watch as she snatched up the receiver. It was 11:02. "Rosco! I was getting worried."

Stony silence met her.

"Rosco?"

"I'm sorry to disappoint you, Annabella."

Belle forced a smile to her lips. "Father! It's nice to hear from you. I didn't expect—"

"It's clear you were anticipating a different messenger, Annabella."

Belle set her shoulders. "Father, what I was trying to say is that I didn't imagine I'd speak to you before your arrival for the wedding."

"That is precisely what I wish to discuss, Annabella."

Her shoulders grew firmer, her spine straighter. *We've been through this conversation already,* she thought. *My "questionable choice in mates," Rosco's "lack of an Ivy League education," his "career." I don't want to participate in this dialogue again.* She changed the subject with a noncommittal, "How is the weather in Florida?"

"Benign."

Belle's expression turned wry. *Benign* was not a condition she would have imagined her father capable of recognizing.

"However, I did not telephone long distance to enter a discourse on meteorology. I phoned to discuss your espousement."

Belle nearly groaned aloud. "I appreciate your concern, Father, but I wish you'd wait and pass judgment after you meet Rosco. He's a fine man, and I love him—"

"Love is not the only ingredient in a marriage, Annabella. . . ."

Belle looked out the rain-gray windows. *That poor dog,* she thought as she half listened to her father's plodding lecture.

". . . I simply ask that you consider this decision thoroughly, Annabella. You made a mistake once before—"

"I *have* considered it, Father."

Silence echoed on both ends of the phone. *Another stalemate,* Belle realized, *one more in an endless line.* She took her eyes off the window and let her glance wander over her office: the foreign-language dictionaries lining the bookcase, the OED, her cherished 1911 *Encyclopedia Britannica.* These were ostensibly the tools of a cryptic-constructor's trade, but they were also a legacy. She'd been raised to value intellect above all other attributes and to believe that the walls of academia were the only foundation that mattered. Those thoughts inevitably carried her to Rayanne and a contemplation on her parental conversations.

"You warned me not to judge a book by its cover, Father. Perhaps, you should wait until you meet Rosco before evaluating him."

The voice on the other end of the line was not amused. "I was referring to scholarly works, Annabella. However, the purpose of my call is to inform you that I may not be able to attend the festivities. My sciatica has been bothering me again, and I fear a long train journey—"

Guilty relief rushed over Belle, but she did her best to temper the reaction. "You could always fly," she offered.

"That's out of the question, I'm afraid, Annabella. You know how little I like airplanes."

"But they're different nowadays, Father. They're far more comfortable—"

"Just as unsafe, however!"

Belle didn't respond to the accusation. Concerning the perils of air travel, her father had always been adamant. "Whatever you feel is best. I wouldn't want you complicating your condition."

The conversation continued for another short minute. There was no more mention of Rosco and no further critique of Belle. Father and daughter concluded in polite formality. "I hope you'll improve quickly," she said.

"It's an arduous trip," was his noncommittal reply.

Belle dropped the receiver back into the cradle and wasn't surprised when it immediately rang again. One of the problems with her insistence upon having a single phone line with no additional services was a frequent busy signal. "Rosco? Sorry, my father called. . . . Where are you? I've been worried. . . ."

The line crackled with static, but no voice was heard.

"Rosco? Your cell phone connection's awful. . . ." She waited for a response. None was forthcoming. "Rosco? Hello?"

Only silence ensued.

"Hello? Rosco?" Belle waited a moment, then banged down the phone, disgruntled. "Why can't telemarketers leave you alone on the weekend?"

CHAPTER

8

The police photographer snapped a series of pictures of the dead woman while Rosco stood near the wall, watching the procedure. The flash ricocheted across the wet asphalt and drenched walls behind the Newcastle bus terminal. With each shot, the twin fire escapes at the rear of the converted nineteenth-century building cast angular shadows along the browned bricks, making the criss-crossed ironwork loom like enormous arachnids.

The flash popped a final time. Even at a distance, Rosco could easily see the woman's face. She seemed far too peaceful, almost as if she were smiling.

"Do they know how she died?" Rosco's question was directed at Abe Jones, who'd arrived at the scene ten minutes before Rosco and Lever.

"I haven't altered the body position. I'm waiting for the ME. He'll have to determine the cause of death." As if he'd been reading Rosco's mind, Jones added, "She looks kind of peaceful, doesn't she?"

"Well, death'll do that for you. . . ." Lever coughed. "Maybe we'll get lucky here. Maybe she died of natural causes . . . just had a heart attack and expired in her sleep. Money or ID?"

Jones shook his head. "Neither . . . I hope you're right about natural causes, but unfortunately, this scene bears a striking resemblance to yesterday's. That's why I thought you should be called before anything was moved . . . day off or not. Sorry, boss." Jones pointed up and down the narrow street. "Like the situation with Freddie, we have a mainly deserted alley—especially after dark—and a body positioned on newspapers: the *Evening Crier* and *Boston Sentinel*. All we're missing is the blood and the dog food."

"And the pint of booze." Lever reached for his cigarettes.

"Right. No booze this time. In fact, the woman doesn't look too badly off. Wet, dirty overalls . . . not what you'd call filthy, though. We have some death stench. . . . That's certainly not her fault. And her boots aren't in great shape, but hey, I've seen far worse."

"A good deal of mud on them," Rosco observed.

"Probably from walking through the park down on Third. I'll take samples and run a comparison."

Lever nodded. "Who found her?"

"The lead came in on the tip line. Anonymously. But that's another reason I wanted the dispatcher to notify you, Al. The call was traced to a pay phone at Eleventh and Hawthorne."

"The *Crier* building?" Rosco asked. Recognizing the location of Belle's office, he made no attempt to mask his surprise.

"Not the actual building," Abe Jones answered. "There's a pay phone on the corner. However, we're talking about eight or nine blocks from here. The person who phoned didn't want to be anywhere near the scene when we arrived. I dispatched one of my men to dust the phone box for prints, but if the caller was cautious enough to establish a credible distance, I doubt we'll find much. I also contacted Sister Mary Catherine at Margaret House Women's Shelter. I figured she and Father Tom have a better handle on Newcastle's street people than anyone. If she doesn't recognize the woman, she should be able to provide other sources."

"Thanks, Abe." Lever turned his attention to Rosco. "Do you know how we get in touch with this Gus character you told me about?"

Rosco shook his head. "No. Apparently, he roams back and forth between here and Boston. Why?"

"Just want to talk, that's all. Maybe he knew her."

"Well, if he's still in Newcastle, my bet is he'll leave as soon as he hears about this."

"Let's not jump to conclusions, Rosco. It's possible she died of natural causes."

"Wishful thinking." Jones nodded toward the end of the alley. "Don't look now, Al, but your hopeful demeanor is about to evaporate."

Rosco and Lever followed Jones's gaze and watched Carlyle plod heavily toward them. He carried a large black case in his right hand, a black umbrella in his left. If he'd had a hood on his coat, he would have looked like the Grim Reaper. When he reached the three men, he said, "What have we got?" No other salutation passed his lips. He gazed perfunctorily at Jones and Lever. Rosco, he completely ignored.

"Dead *Jane* Doe this time," Lever answered. "I was hoping the causes might be natural."

Carlyle remained standing while he scanned the scene in silence. He glanced up at the bus depot roof, briefly allowing the rain exposure to his face, then returned his gaze to the alley. *"Natural cause* is not a term I'd use, Al. . . . Homicide would be more like it. I don't think the subject could have fallen—or jumped—and landed in this position. Partially under the fire escape, lying on newspapers?" Carlyle shook his head. "Don't even hope for suicide. Looks like she'd made herself a bed same as our victim yesterday."

He placed his case on the wet pavement, slipped on a pair of surgical gloves, and crouched over the body. "Vertebral column . . . neural arch . . ." He looked at his watch and made a note. "Odd . . . but interesting coloration. The bruise is nearly dissipated. . . . Do you have a name? Address?"

Lever shook his head.

"Money? Valuables?"

This time Abe Jones responded. "Nothing. We could be looking at a robbery gone sour."

"No signs of struggle, Abe. . . . The face is calm."

"Rosco and I noted that, too."

Carlyle stiffened slightly but otherwise didn't react. He continued as if Rosco's name hadn't been mentioned. "I'm not liking this skin color. . . . Something doesn't jibe. Clearly we have a crushed cervical vertebra. This lady was put out like a light."

"Could she have been killed while she was sleeping?" Rosco asked. "Hit on the back of the head? Something like that?"

The medical examiner didn't reply.

"What about it, Carlyle?" Lever asked.

"Possible but not probable. Your attacker would have to have a thorough understanding of human anatomy . . . a martial arts expert, maybe. *Maybe.* But again, not probable. If our gal were sleeping, her skull would have been in a similar relationship to the ground as it is here. . . . There's little to no flexibility in the spine—"

"So you're saying there's no way it could have been an accident?" Lever's voice was weary; he still hoped he wouldn't have to open a second homicide file in as many days.

"Not from my initial examination. The autopsy could prove me wrong. *Maybe.*" Carlyle retrieved his umbrella from Jones and said, "I'll get the van." He headed up the alley, passing Sister Mary Catherine and a uniformed officer. Carlyle scarcely acknowledged them.

When the nun reached Lever, Al extended his hand. "Thanks for coming, Sister. I believe you already know Rosco Polycrates, Belle Graham's fiancé, and this is Abe Jones, the department's forensics expert. . . . And this person—" he pointed to the corpse—"is why we're here. Does she look familiar?"

Sister Mary Catherine took a reflexive step backward, then walked forward and knelt beside the body, crossing herself before whispering a few words into the dead woman's ear.

"I'm sorry to be so blunt," Lever said. "But do you think you might recognize her?"

The nun stood and attempted to brush the dampness from her knees. "No . . . I've never seen her before. She's never entered Margaret House."

"Not even for a meal? You're sure?"

"I remember everyone who comes through our doors,

Lieutenant." Sister Mary Catherine smiled gently and looked at Rosco. "I'm sure our volunteers remember them, as well."

"Can you refer us to another agency—"

The nun shook her head. "This woman was not homeless, Lieutenant. She was not living on the streets. I'm sure your medical examiner will come to the same conclusion."

"You seem pretty sure of that fact, Sister."

Again, the peaceable smile. "I am."

"Then would you care to take a stab at why she was sleeping on newspapers in an alley behind a bus station and had no money on her?"

Sister Mary Catherine studied Lever, an expression of growing comprehension and compassion on her quiet face. "I appreciate your concern, Lieutenant, and the strain you must feel . . . especially given yesterday's situation, but I've spent my life among the lost and hopeless, whether children or adults. Their faces are like road maps, showing each path taken, each disappointment, each mistake, each unfulfilled hope. This unfortunate woman did not live on the streets."

"Okay, but—"

"I've said a prayer for her, and for you and your team of police officers, as well. There's nothing else I can offer you. Now, if someone could drive me back to the mission, I would appreciate it. I apologize if I seem brusque, but I have a great deal of work . . . among the living." She touched Lever's arm in tranquil finality. "Of course, I will be available at Margaret House if you want to question me further . . . or should you wish to talk with some of our residents."

Lever's glance moved from the nun to the dead woman and back again. He didn't speak for a moment; when he did, his tone was solemn. "Thank you for your time, Sister . . . and for your prayers." Then he nodded to the officer who'd originally escorted the nun to the scene. As the two walked purposefully away, they passed Carlyle's van backing down the alley; Sister Mary Catherine briefly placed her hand on the vehicle's dark metallic side.

The medical examiner took another fifteen minutes to finish his on-site examination and load the body onto his van. He worked in perfunctory silence, but before leaving the scene, he spoke to Lever while giving a conspicuous nod in Rosco's direction. "Would you like to hear my initial thoughts or should I wait until we've returned to headquarters and dispensed with nondepartmental personnel?"

Lever sighed. He'd been through this routine before. When Rosco had been NPD, he and Carlyle had had a number of disagreements. The medical examiner resented Rosco's unconventional methods; Rosco often considered Carlyle's work sloppy; he felt the city deserved better. To top it off, Rosco's assessments had a sneaky way of being correct.

But Lever needed to keep peace, and at the moment, Carlyle was the one who required attention. "Take a hike, will you, Polly—crates? But don't leave the scene. I want to learn more about this Gus character."

Rosco walked to the end of the alley, then strolled into the bus depot and had a chat with with the newspaper vendor. He bought a copy of the *Boston Sentinel*. By the time he'd returned to the alley, Carlyle had left.

"So?" he said to Lever.

"What do you think, Polly—crates? Carlyle had nothing new to add. Just that he thinks you're a class-A jerk. He wanted to take this opportunity to reiterate his words of wisdom."

"This is interesting. . . ." Jones said as he crouched to examine the area where the body had been. "The victim's head was resting on today's issue of the *Boston Sentinel*. The *Crier* copies are all old, but the Boston paper's new. If we fixed the hour the bus depot newsstand opens, we might be able to narrow our time of death."

It was Rosco who answered. "The newsstand's a twenty-four-hour operation. The *Sentinel* comes down from Boston between four-thirty and five every morning except Sundays. The current vendor doesn't remember a homeless woman in overalls, but he didn't start work until eight A.M. . . . Of course, she could have pulled the paper out of the trash or gotten it from the coin box on the corner. That information's from the vendor, not me." Rosco handed a slip of paper to Lever. "But just in case she didn't get it from the coin box, here's the home phone of the guy who had the midnight-to-eight shift last night."

"I'm glad to see you've been using your time wisely, Polly—crates."

CHAPTER

9

B elle was staring disconsolately into a near-empty kitchen cabinet when the doorbell rang. She grabbed a can of condensed mushroom soup, plopped it on the counter, and called out, "Just a sec!" as she hurried through the house.

Rosco stood at the door, a newspaper tucked under his arm.

Belle kissed him. She was so focused on her own thoughts that she failed to notice the paper or Rosco's curious expression. "Al didn't need you any longer?"

"I told him everything I knew about Gus and Freddie, Sara's peripheral involvement, vis-à-vis the dog . . . the works. . . . Sister Mary Catherine came by the scene at Lever's request. She had a strong belief that the dead woman had not been living on the streets."

Belle nodded thoughtfully. "You know, I feel a certain relief that this latest death isn't part of a serial crime. In the back of my mind, I've been wondering if the city's more questionable vested interests could be ratcheting up for a war against the homeless shelters."

Rosco changed the subject. "Have you had lunch yet?"

They walked to the kitchen, hands touching. "We can warm some mushroom soup," she said. "And I've got saltines. We could melt cheese over the crackers. . . ."

"Sounds great." Rosco placed the newspaper on the counter. "Sorry to be late. I really did try to call earlier, but the line was constantly busy—"

"My father decided it was time for one final diatribe." She opened the soup can and unceremoniously dumped the contents into a pot.

"He loves you, Belle. He's expressing his feelings the only way he knows how."

"I agree with the *latter* part of your assessment, Rosco."

He turned her around to face him and slipped his arms around her shoulders. "I don't care what he thinks of me, my education, family, work . . . but I *do* care about you. I love you, and I'm going to marry you . . . and you are the only person I'm trying to please. Now and always."

Belle gazed up into his eyes. "You're the best guy on earth," she said. "I hope you know that."

"We're not our families, Belle."

"I know."

"Or our friends."

"Well, *friends* . . . now, that's *different.*" She gave him a grateful kiss, then moved away and opened the refrigerator door. "No milk! Oh, drat! I'll have to thin this stuff with water. One of these days, I have to learn some basic culinary skills."

"Such as buying milk?"

"Very funny. I was thinking more in terms of creating meals from scratch."

"Your deviled eggs are excellent—"

"That's only one dish, Rosco. It's not enough to keep body and soul alive. Anyway, they're more of an hors d'oeuvre than a meal."

She stirred the soup dreamily. "Oh, I forgot! We had some excellent news! I was waiting till I saw you to share it. A thumbs-up from Captain Lancia. We're definitely getting married in Newcastle waters, so we can get our license first thing Monday morning. Lancia can't officiate, but Sara is contacting a JP she knows. Her initial suggestion was a real-life *Washington judge,* but I nixed the idea, which took some doing, as you can imagine. *Il capitáno* came to the rescue. His ministrations lessened Sara's disappointment at not being able to phone her dear friend on the Supreme Court. If Lancia ever loses his job on the *Akbar*, he can always become a gigolo—"

"You've been busy."

"You don't know the half of it. If Sara had her way, she'd organize every aspect of our wedding . . . and maybe play both roles, too." Belle paused and regarded Rosco thoughtfully. "I'm sorry you've been involved in this police business. It doesn't make for an easy prenuptial week. Besides, I've missed you."

"I've missed you, too."

"No trace of Carson's dog, I take it?" she asked.

"I contacted the Humane Society and all local veterinarians. They swore they'd call me before they . . . well, did anything drastic. We just have to wait."

Belle left the soup pot, returned to the fridge, and retrieved a wedge of Cheddar cheese, which she began slicing, laying thin strips atop a number of crackers. Her expression was pensive; it was clear her thoughts weren't on her work. "I wouldn't like to be lost and hungry," she said, then added a typical non sequitur, "Paprika, do you think?"

"Not as much as last time."

Belle's eyes narrowed into bemused slits. "The last time I used cayenne, by mistake. Paprika's not as spicy. . . ."

As she perused her selection of spices, Rosco unfolded the newspaper. *"Hideaway,"* he muttered as if to himself, "four letters . . ."

Unconsciously Belle replied. "Nest, cave, hole, lair . . ."

"Tongue?" Rosco prodded.

"Language, organ of taste or speech, dialect—"

"Six letters."

"Accent . . . lingua . . . What are you up to?" Belle turned around and stared at the newspaper. "Since when have you started doing the crossword in the *Boston Sentinel*? 5-Across: *Hideaway.*" Her fingers pointed to the puzzle grid. "Thus your LAIR . . . and LINGUA for *Tongue* at 5-Down, making *Mr. Amin* IDI, of course, and *Ms. Parks* ROSA." Belle chuckled. "Oh, and 16, 30, 51 and 65-Across run the full length of the puzzle grid. This looks intriguing . . . and nicely symmetrical. . . ."

Rosco took a beat. "Look at 1-Across. *Anagram for—*"

"Anagram for 75-Across," Belle muttered. Her eyes darted across the clues. "75-Across: *Retreats* . . . four letters . . . *Retreat* is both noun and verb. A monk's cell could be a retreat, likewise a desert isle; to flee is a form of retreating. However, in plural, the words would be five letters. . . . Wait, I've got it! SPAS. The anagram of which is either ASPS, PASS, or SAPS."

Rosco paused again. "The dead woman was found with a copy of today's *Sentinel* under her head. It was open to the comics page. The crossword is at the foot of that section."

"I know," was Belle's wary reply.

"That's why I purchased the paper. . . . There may be a connection here." He pushed the *Sentinel* across the counter toward her, but she made no move to take it. *"Anagram* is part of the first clue . . . like your nickname—"

Belle interrupted. "Rosco, we're getting married one week from today."

"I know we are."

"So, what does that mean?"

"That you don't want to discuss crime in Newcastle."

She nodded her head. "It's not our business, Rosco. Really, it isn't."

Inadvertently, his eyes drifted back to the newspaper. "But doesn't it seem unusual for a Boston daily to be found at the scene—?"

"The city's less than an hour away—"

"And open to the crossword—?"

Belle's expression remained unmoving. "A coincidence. That's all. What does Al think?"

"He didn't notice the puzzle. Neither did Abe. . . . Come on, Belle, humor me. This might have some bearing on the case. Call it one of my hunches. . . . But the woman's torso was lying atop *old* Newcastle papers, her head resting on *today's Sentinel*. In Carson's case, there were also newspapers that had been used as a bed—"

"But you just said the situations were unrelated—"

"You *inferred* that, Belle, when I told you Sister Mary Catherine didn't believe the dead woman had been living on the streets."

Belle thought. "I have enormous respect for the nuns, but it's certainly *possible* that's a mistaken assumption. Perhaps the dead woman had only recently taken to the streets. . . . Maybe she arrived here by bus last night, so as not to be seen begging in her former hometown. . . . Pride plays an important role in all our lives, whatever our financial circumstances."

Rosco didn't reply.

Belle frowned and then sighed, the sound a mixture of frustration and guilt. "Rosco, I don't want to deal with this. I don't want to worry about Father Tom and the nuns. I'm being selfish, I know, but for the coming week, all I want to concentrate on is getting married, having a pleasant celebration, and beginning a new life together."

"There may well be linkages between the two deaths—"

She touched Rosco's arm and looked into his face. "If there are, Al will discover them. And if they turn out to involve the city's criminal element, the NPD will handle it."

"Fill in the puzzle, Belle. It will only take a minute."

"And then we can forget the entire situation?"

"If there are no clues pertaining to the deaths—"

Belle attempted a jest. "Not good enough. . . . I'll make you a deal. First we eat. *Then* we ink in the crossword. Any linkages go to Al. Okay?"

Across

1. 75-Across anagram
5. Hideaway
9. Ms. James
13. Remove
14. Chinese lead-in
15. Cheat
16. Walston "Damn Yankees" role?
19. Judge Lance
20. Oxygen tanker ltrs.
21. King lead-in
22. "Could———Be Magic"
24. Cow chomp?
26. Smells
30. Like a Barbie doll?
34. Roman sun god
35. Perrier, e.g.
36. Ms. McIntire
37. Batter's stat.
40. School grp.
42. Logos, abbr.
44. Not pos.
45. "———hook Up?"
47. Sick
49. Travel org.
51. Detectives' traits
57. Mends
58. ———la-la
59. Track tip
60. Spanish article
62. April 15th grp.
64. Power proj.
65. Hanoi Hilton competitor?
71. Shocked
72. Mr. Perkins
73. Overjoy
74. Vegas tip
75. Retreats
76. TV rooms

Down

1. Ms. Franklin
2. ———-faire
3. Tire fig.
4. Deal in
5. Tongue
6. "Frankie———Johnny"
7. Mr. Amin
8. Ms. Parks
9. Quito country
10. Dent lead-in
11. McCort novel
12. Mr. Lincoln
13. Ms. Wharton
17. How Gaelic tales were told
18. Luminosity
23. '60s protest grp.
25. White House mono.
27. Sign
28. Playwright David
29. Catch
31. "At the———"
32. Consume
33. Home of Ding Dong Daddy
37. Hasty
38. "———Suede Shoes"
39. Ingrid in "Casablanca"
41. The Greatest
43. Dooley in "Casablanca"
46. Indulge oneself
48. "Whole———of Shakin' Goin On"
50. River isle
52. "———It a Pity"
53. Wild Asian sheep
54. No way to return from Aruba?
55. Comforters
56. Tired
61. Basics
63. Cast off

KING'S RANSOM

65. Tam
66. Self
67. Thumbs up!
68. Music choice
69. Pitcher's stat.
70. Bravo!

C H A P T E R

10

"But what about 65-Across?" Rosco insisted. Tenacity kept him on his feet; he leaned over Belle as she finished inking in the *Sentinel* crossword. "Or 30-Across, for Pete's sake?"

Belle put down her red Bic pen and gave him a long, indulgent look. "It's a theme puzzle, Rosco. Look at the title. 'King's Ransom.' Constructors have a field day creating them. You take names of flowers or world capitals, movie stars, anything . . . and find inventive ways of—"

"Come on, Belle. . . . First of all, I don't like anything with the word *ransom* in it. And look at 65-Across. You've got to see the connection there."

"HEARTBREAK HOTEL? The answer merely follows the Elvis Presley theme. And I've got to add that the person responsible for this crossword did an excellent job. "BLUE *Suede Shoes*, which also references CARL *Perkins*, who recorded the same song and is found at 72-Across. . . .

Frankie AND *Johnny . . .* ALL *Shook Up . . .* For cleverness, I liked that solution the best—"

"But Heartbreak Hotel was what Gus Taylor called the Saint Augustine Mission—"

"And the clue here is *Hanoi Hilton competitor,* providing a brainy bit of historical allusion. This is an interesting and challenging crossword, Rosco, but that's all it is. Nothing points to murder. And nothing remotely alludes to a serial crime or—"

Rosco groaned in frustration. "30-Across," he said. "HARDHEADED WOMAN. We have an unidentified female victim. Carlyle's initial estimate on cause of death was—"

Belle interrupted. "And what's the clue?"

"Like a Barbie doll?"

She tilted her head in amusement. "I love you, Rosco, and I wish I could agree that this cryptic had some bearing on that poor woman's death, but I think we're just grasping at straws."

"But *Anagram,* Belle! That's your nickname, right there in 1-Across!"

"Uh-huh. And we have *Detectives' traits* at 51-Across. And EDITH *Wharton* at 13-Down and *Playwright David* RABE at 28-Down. I don't mean to be glib, but the only hidden connections I can find are the king of rock and roll and literary lions, which are also kings of their own particular jungles."

Rosco let out a resigned sigh and walked to the window. Almost miraculously, the sodden clouds of the prior two days had disappeared, leaving in their wake young grass so brilliantly green it stung the senses and an afternoon sky wafting with hope and golden light. "It was worth a shot," he said.

"It was," Belle agreed, then added an affectionate, "Al and Abe and Carlyle are working these cases, Rosco. Your job is to get married."

"I spotted that *Anagram*, right away. . . ."

Belle cocked an eyebrow. "You never did explain how a puzzle klutz like you constructed a crossword marriage proposal. MARRY ME BELLE; I LOVE YOU DEAR. That was quite impressive."

"That's for me to know and you to find out."

Belle chuckled. "Oh, I'll find out, all right."

Rosco caught himself grinning from ear to ear. "How about we drive to the beach, take a long, slow walk, and then have supper at the Athena?"

Belle sighed, but the sound was full of yearning. "How about we visit Cleo first, check on her kitchen's progress—or lack thereof—and then take a solitary stroll?"

"We'll never get out of Cleo's house without staying for dinner."

"You said we weren't our families, Rosco."

"Right . . . but walking into Cleo's house is a little like joining the Marines. You may have *entered* voluntarily, but *leaving* is another story; you're not going anywhere until your tour is up."

The phone rang. Instinctively, Rosco grabbed it, barking a quick, "Yup?" into the receiver. Simultaneously, Belle reached for it, a mixture of astonishment tinged with indignation on her face. "Hello?" Rosco announced. "Hello?" He dropped the receiver back into the cradle. "Phone sales . . . The person didn't even have the courtesy to speak."

"Did it occur to you that the call might have been for me?" Despite her smile, Belle's tone was cool.

Rosco attempted a joke. "If a man answers, hang up?"

"That's not what I meant, Rosco . . . but . . . well, this is my home, you know."

"And soon to be shared, right?"

They remained silent for a minute, both suddenly engrossed in the magnitude of the adjustment they were anticipating. It was as if neither Belle nor Rosco had fully focused on the issue of joining two households before. Belle pictured her quiet little habits forever altered: working till all hours in her ancient and beloved terry cloth robe, dictionaries and encyclopedias lying open at her feet, a licorice stick dangling half-consumed in her hand; while Rosco envisioned the morning silence of his brisk routine: talk radio with The I-Man, a jog, a shower, the first jolt of coffee . . . all irretrievably transformed into chatty domesticity.

Then apprehension gave way to reflection. Rosco broke the ice. "Are we talking about phone etiquette here or something bigger?"

Belle thought, then reached for his hand. "Phone etiquette . . ."

"What do you say we discuss that over a candle-lit dinner?"

"I thought you said Cleo wouldn't allow us to desert her," Belle teased.

"I'm marrying *you*, Belle, not the Marines."

Sharon was in tears when Belle and Rosco pulled up to Cleo's driveway. "I can't tell you how sorry I am," she kept saying, her big face livid with anguish. "I thought Geoff had a grip on the damn thing. . . ."

Cleo, torn between ire and sympathy, merely shook her head and stared at the badly dented cardboard crate lying in her drive. Geoffrey Wright's pickup truck loomed to one side with its owner standing irresolutely near the tailgate. "We'll order another," he said. "It's no big deal."

Cleo's response was waspish. "And *when* will *that* arrive?"

The usually take-charge artisan thought for a moment before offering a noncommittal, "We can put a rush on the order."

"I've ruined Belle's wedding!" Sharon moaned. It was at that moment that Belle stepped out of Rosco's Jeep. Her heart flip-flopped when she heard the words; she tried to smile, but the effort felt sticky and false.

"What happened?" she finally managed.

Cleo turned to her future sister-in-law. "Geoffrey and Sharon drove over to Ace Plumbing and Electrical to pick up the *new* dishwasher. They came back. Prepared to *unload*. And *voilà!* The top-of-the-line *Miele* that's been *back-ordered* for almost two *months* fell off the truck."

"It was my fault," Sharon said. "I thought Geoff had—"

Rosco looked at the three women's stricken faces. "It's just a dishwasher, right? We're not talking a broken hip."

Sharon began crying afresh, while Cleo gave her brother a nasty glance. "It's the *one* piece of kitchen equipment we've been *waiting* for, Rosco. Without it, the refurbishment simply *can't* proceed. Sorry, Belle. We'll have to make *other* arrangements for the party. Maybe Ariadne can . . . No, her home is *far* too cramped—"

"We can use paper plates, Cleo," Rosco offered. "Nothing to wash. No muss or fuss—"

Cleo's response was biting. "We can't leave a vast *hole* in the *cabinetry,* Rosco. There's no countertop!"

Sharon echoed a similar objection: "I can't finish laying marble without all the major appliances in place. I won't risk chipping my stone trying to slide the dishwasher under it."

Belle said nothing.

"Sorry for the setback, Tinker Bell," Geoffrey Wright finally proffered, then reiterated his hopes that a replacement machine could be found. "Maybe by midweek," he said.

"That simply isn't *possible,*" Cleo interrupted. "The Miele was *back-ordered—*"

"From the factory, Cleo. From the factory. But, when stock finally reaches the wholesalers, it doesn't take a genius to scare up another model."

Cleo's face remained grim, but Sharon's brightened considerably. "I'll go back to Vermont for a couple of days, make sure the lambs are okay and the barn still standing. We can start fresh on Wednesday . . . Thursday, at the latest. By Saturday, I'm sure we'll have—"

Belle finally spoke. "Perhaps we should arrange to have the party at my house, Cleo. With a little effort we could—"

But Rosco's sister wouldn't hear of the suggestion. "I wouldn't *dream* of welcoming you into the Polycrates family without throwing a big Greek *bash.* Don't worry Tinker Bell, we'll get this worked out if it kills us all in the process."

CHAPTER

11

Carlyle was in his element. For one thing, it was approaching noon on Sunday, and he'd been ensconced in the basement autopsy room of the Newcastle Police Department since well before seven A.M. For another, he'd been examining the city's most recent homicide victim, an *unidentified* body, to boot, and one where the cause of death wasn't as obvious as a cobblestone to the head. The third piece of this satisfactory equation was that Carlyle was not alone. Al Lever was in the morgue with him, having been forced to relinquish his treasured Sunday morning tee time in favor of this chummy tête-à-tête. That solitary fact provided Carlyle with more than a little sadistic glee.

He smiled to himself as he stared at the cadaver lying blue and exposed on an icy metal table, then jotted a few notes in quick, cribbed shorthand, and finally resumed eating a cheeseburger with his ungloved left hand. Droplets of ketchup threatened to spill from the greasy, yellow paper.

"Good," he said, although it was abundantly clear to Al Lever that the medical examiner's pleasure was not derived from the folks at the local Burger King.

"I don't know how you can do that," Lever said. He was smoking furiously. Veteran cop though he was, Al couldn't stomach the smell of the autopsy room. *Methane gas and butyric acid,* he told himself repeatedly; *they're natural; they're organic compounds.* But the exhortation did nothing to dispel the churning of his stomach. Lever took another long drag on his cigarette and reiterated his comments on Carlyle's peculiar dining habits.

"Hmmm?" The medical examiner didn't look up.

"Eat . . . ? I don't know how you can eat that stuff down here."

Carlyle gave Lever the briefest of glances. "Yeah," he admitted, "burgers gets cold real fast in the lab. I shouldn't have bolted the fries first, but hell, they're no fun cold, either . . . one of life's unpleasant little decisions." He opened his mouth for another mammoth bite, chewed and swallowed noisily, then returned to perusing his clipboard.

"Yep. Blunt trauma," he announced smugly. "Just as I surmised during my initial examination." He polished off the cheeseburger, crushed its tomato-speckled wrapper, and wiped his fingers on a paper napkin, which he then rather fussily balled up and disposed of with a slam dunk into a corner trash can. The attention given to tidying away his meal seemed disproportionate to his concern for the corpse. Lever sensed an unwillingness on Carlyle's part to make eye contact.

"X rays don't lie, Lieutenant. Especially when we can zap 'em with those deep, fifteen-minute exposures. Nice not to worry about radiation overload, not on folks who are already demised. Bottom line: your lady took a hard whack from behind. A relatively quick death, like I said. Hanging can be a lot messier. People don't like to admit it, but that's the truth—"

"So we can rule out any possibility of strangulation?"

"Absolutely." Carlyle chuckled, keeping his gaze lowered but shaking his head from side to side as if he were dealing with a fifth-grader.

Al focused on the tube lights that hung in pairs throughout the room; he concentrated on the independent ventilation system, the security locks, the motion detectors; what he avoided was the pervasive odors of human remains, fried hamburger meat, and greasy fries.

"Could the weapon have been similar to the one that killed Freddie Carson? A cobblestone, a brick, possibly a tire jack?"

"You found a tire jack at the scene?" Carlyle asked, finally allowing his eyes to meet Lever's.

"No, it's just something that popped into my head."

"Well, it could've been a jack handle maybe, but there's no way this was done with a brick or stone; otherwise, we would've had skin abrasions, blood. . . ." Carlyle pointed at the corpse. "The weapon made contact here, at the base of the skull. We've got eight pairs of cervical nerves protected by the first few cervical vertebrae. You crush one of those bones, and the party's over. Whatever did the damage was round and smooth, like a pipe or something. Jones lifted hair samples from the nape of her neck for analysis. . . ." Carlyle shrugged. "Everything leaves a trail . . . a footprint. It may take Abe a few days, but he'll be able to determine if the weapon was a baseball bat, a tire jack, or a golf club. I hear tell golfers can be touchy people."

Lever didn't rise to the bait. Instead, he stubbed out his

cigarette in a glass petri dish that had been designated as morgue ashtray. "I'm trying to make a connection here, Carlyle. Are we looking at a serial situation? Someone who's stalking individuals bedded down on the streets for the night? Both cases involved blows to the head—"

"Who knows? Speculating on motive and method isn't my field. But you get two people without ID turning up dead in deserted areas of Newcastle on two consecutive days. . . . If you and your boys don't make the connection, you can bet the newspapers will. . . . But, hey, why not ask Polycrates? I'll bet he has plenty of thoughts on the subject . . . for what they're worth." True to form, Carlyle had grown truculent in a second. He resumed concentrating on the body lying on the table.

"Time of death?"

Carlyle's ghoulish smile flickered to life. "Well, that's another tricky issue, Lever. Algor mortis? Usually we're talking a drop of—give or take—one degree Celsius per hour—"

Lever interrupted, "English, please, Carlyle."

"A body cools down at a fairly predictable rate. Around here, this time of year, we can count on about two degrees *Fahrenheit* an hour."

"And . . . ?"

"Well, this gal was stone cold when I arrived at the bus station, which confused me somewhat. Obviously, rigor mortis had come and gone. I suppose I should have picked that up at the scene, but I was fooled by the date on the *Sentinel* . . . which, I think we all were. . . ." Again, his eyes darted around the room but avoided Lever. "My point being: this lady was dead long before that newspaper you found under her head was ever printed."

"What?!"

"Jones said the daily *Sentinel* rolls into town at four . . . five A.M., correct?"

Lever nodded.

"Jane Doe here was discovered Saturday morning, with her head resting on *Saturday's* paper, but my calculations now put her death thirty-six to forty-eight hours earlier, maybe longer. Rigor mortis sets in after about six hours, disappears usually in thirty. My tissue analysis revealed a presence of adipocere; it's a substance that's formed during the decomposition of the body, and—"

"But then how did the Saturday *Sentinel* get—?"

"I'm just the ME, Lieutenant. I ain't no detective, but common sense says Miss Doe didn't die behind the bus station. . . . She was kept on ice for a while and dumped there."

When Belle's doorbell rang, she was in the process of scooping the last remaining tablespoonful of a whipped mayonnaise and egg yolk filling from a red glass bowl and sliding it into a twelfth hard-boiled egg white. She called out, "Just be a minute," as she licked the mixture from her fingertips and smiled at her handiwork: a dozen perfect deviled eggs. Who could ask for a more glorious luncheon? She crossed to the kitchen sink, rinsed off her hands, and walked to her front door, happily flicking a dish towel as she went.

"Sorry," she said, opening the paneled outer door, "I was cooking . . . well, not really cooking, but—"

There was no one there.

Belle undid the latch on her screen door and peered across an empty porch toward the street. Not a soul was in sight; not a person strolling by, not a car, not a truck, only three robins diligently scratching for worms in her front yard.

"Hello . . . ?" she called. "Hello?"

She stepped out onto the porch and almost fell over a long white flower box extravagantly beribboned in blue and cream. It was a package that shouted, *A dozen long-stem roses.*

Belle bent down, lifted the box into her arms, and removed the greeting card from its miniature envelope. It read, *"For Belle, from a Secret Admirer."*

"Rosco?" she called. "Rosco . . . ? I made deviled eggs." With no response, she raised her voice. "You're going to get hungry lurking around in the shrubbery!"

Again, she was greeted by absolute silence. Belle chuckled. "You're a swell guy!" she sang out. "And one terrific fiancé! I'm leaving the door open just in case you turn peckish."

Humming to herself, she walked back inside with her prize. "Hmmm, feels a little light," she murmured as she reentered the kitchen, set the box on the counter, and then noted with dismay that the white cardboard had been nicked in several places as if badly jostled in delivery. *I hope the flowers are okay,* she thought as she carefully slid the ribbon aside and pulled off the lid. Nestled in a bed of green tissue paper lay neither rose nor spray of lilac nor exotic orchid stems. What she found instead was a neatly hand-drawn crossword puzzle.

Belle shook her head and smiled afresh. "Another of Rosco's romantic inventions . . . although I think I would have preferred flowers."

Across

1. Room
5. Mountain———
8. Peruses
13. "The———and I"
14. WWII theater
15. Possible
16. Teen tack-on
17. ———Lanka
18. Legal excuse
19. Center of Florida?
21. Pericles finale
22. Interrogator
25. Basil sauce
27. Shoe size
30. Neck wreath
31. Oklahoma town
33. Kitchen meas.
34. Deli choice
36. Made a lap
37. Chocolate———
38. Vadim film
41. Espy
42. Sgt. Bilko, e.g.
43. Plowright film
45. Neth. neighbor
46. Traveling music?
48. Fuss
49. Fool
50. Certain blades
51. "Psycho III," e.g.
53. Seaweed
55. Ray Lawrence film
57. "The———Thief," Nichetti comedy
59. Tic-tac-toe winner
60. Char
64. Hurried
65. Select
66. Writer Bombeck
67. Put in a new lawn
68. New Zealand parrot
69. Superman's vision

Down

1. Alias
2. Semi
3. Vane position
4. Comply
5. Ancestor, abbr.
6. Half of an Agnieszka Holland film title
7. Dramatist's diary
8. Gat
9. Bridge position
10. Seagal film
11. Sixth-century date
12. Yen unit
15. Lumet film
20. Film trailer
22. Pacino and others
23. Construction battalion
24. Kubrick film
26. Heap
28. "Star Trek" division
29. Sixth sense
32. O'Toole's film debut
35. Roger
37. Rebel org.
39. Land plot
40. Oasts
41. Golfer's org.
44. Negative conjunction
46. Like a prison
47. Leaning
52. Flynn role
54. Reverberation
56. Bit
57. Second, abbr.
58. Pool stick

JUST THE BEGINNING

61. Goof
62. Med. grp.
63. Actor Aldo

"'Just the Beginning,'" Belle murmured with an easy smile. "A clever title for a prewedding cryptic." Unconsciously, she began humming and then singing a show tune from the Broadway musical *Gypsy*. When she reached the climax—and the puzzle's complimentary phrase—she gave a loud, Ethel Merman flourish. "Everything's coming up roses," she sang out the song's title, then thought, how appropriate! I've got to find out who created this crossword for Rosco. He's being awfully cagey with his little secret.

Completely forgetting the deviled eggs, she hurried into her office with the puzzle, then grabbed her red pen. "Film titles . . . This is going to be fun. . . ." She murmured to herself as she worked. "6-Down: *Half of an Agnieszka Holland film title* . . . The answer is EUROPA; 10-Down's solution is ABOVE THE LAW; 15-Down: DEATH TRAP . . ." Belle paused. Well-constructed though it was, the crossword was beginning to feel unsettling. 38-Across: BLOOD AND ROSES.

A chill ran down her spine; she put down her pen and stared at the paper before her. Similar and ominous messages appeared at 24-Down and 32-Down. She mouthed silent words while her brain made a quick leap to a frightening conclusion. The puzzle wasn't an ingenious gift from Rosco; it was an angry, perhaps even threatening message, and it had been hand-delivered to her. *DEATH TRAP,* she thought. *BLOOD AND ROSES. KILLER'S KISS* . . . *A crossword packed in an empty florist's box.* Belle grabbed the phone and punched in Rosco's number. "Can you meet me at Lawson's?" she said the moment he'd picked up the receiver.

Rosco noticed the tension in her voice instantly; any possible jests about her ritual Sunday time-out died in his throat. "What's wrong?"

"Someone planted a crossword in a flower box and left it on my—" Her voice broke off suddenly. "Oh, jeez! I left the door open!"

"Belle! Wait! What's going on?"

But the line was dead.

"Do me a favor, don't do that to me again, okay? You had me worried sick, Belle. I called right back, but you'd obviously left the phone off the hook. I didn't know what to think."

Belle stretched her hand across the scarred cherry-pink Formica, which matched every other banquette table at Lawson's coffee shop, and touched Rosco's fingers. The two were facing each other and leaning so far forward their heads nearly met. Between them, a pair of laminated menus lay forgotten.

"I'm sorry. I didn't think. I'd assumed the roses were

from you, and that you were outside waiting for me to finish the crossword. Then I started filling in the answers, and I realized . . ."

Rosco squeezed her hand. "Tell me again what happened. From the beginning."

She recommenced her tale, inserting every detail she could recall.

Rosco interrupted briefly. "Was there a florist's name attached to the card? Or on the box?"

"I didn't look. I assumed it was a gift from you. It was a white box. Dented and nicked in places . . . I remember being concerned that the flowers had been damaged. . . ."

"Go on."

"I shouldn't have left the door wide open like that."

Rosco paused before replying; his expression was grim. "No, you shouldn't. You've gotten too much media attention, and we've joked about it, but . . . Even that headline from the British paper? 'Cryptics Queen Clues Coppers,' or something like that? To say nothing of the interview in *Personality* magazine. It's definitely the kind of notoriety that could make an unbalanced mind fixate on you . . ." Rosco didn't finish the thought. Instead, he said, "Let's look at the crossword together. You were talking so fast I didn't take in everything you said."

"Sit beside me, okay?" Belle's voice was soft.

Rosco attempted a lighthearted retort. "What will Martha say?"

As if she'd been awaiting her cue, the waitress appeared, her blond hairdo lacquered to perfection, her uniform rustling with determination. "Okay, you two lovebirds. Break it up." Stuck into her frozen tresses was a pencil, which she removed to write their order. "What'll it be?"

"We haven't looked at the menu yet." Rosco's tone was duly apologetic; Martha was a force to be reckoned with.

She sighed mightily, the underwiring beneath the pink nylon facade creaking and groaning. "I'll get you what you always order. Grilled cheese for my man; French toast for the lady." She snatched up the menus before either Rosco or Belle had time to reply and bustled off, calling over her shoulder, "Your pal Lever should do something about this city, Rosco. It's a sin when homeless folks are murdered in their sleep. They got enough trouble without waking up dead."

Belle's worried face relaxed in a wan smile. "Perhaps Al should ask Martha to find the criminals. She obviously knows everything else that's going on in this town."

"Somehow, I can't picture her and Al working well together."

Belle chuckled. "Maybe it's imagining that confetti-colored uniform bouncing around in his unmarked brown police car."

"I don't think the car's the issue."

Both remained silent for a moment while the diner's congenial Sunday hum circled around them: the eager chatter of children and grandparents, teenage girls giggling in fits and starts, a party of elderly men who finished each other's jokes and stories. There was the clatter of restaurant crockery, the plink of warm spoons, waitresses calling to the fry cook, and the old-fashioned bell above the door that jangled exuberantly at each entrance and exit.

Rosco left his seat and slid in beside Belle. "Do you want to show me the crossword now or wait?"

Without replying, Belle pulled the hand-drawn puzzle from her purse. " 'Just the Beginning,' " she said, pointing to the heading. "I thought it was a wonderful title." Her finger pointed to thematic clues. "It's film oriented . . . and very well done: directors, actors, actresses. The clue for the long one at 7-Down is *Dramatist's diary*; the solution is WRITERS NOTEBOOK. 20-Down is *Film trailer,* which is a PROMO, but then look at these solutions." Belle's hand hovered above the paper. "24-Down . . . and 32-Down . . ."

"KILLERS KISS," Rosco read aloud. "KIDNAPPED." He sat up straight; his gaze strayed to the window, to the parked cars in the street, the few pedestrians sauntering by. "I'm not getting a good feeling about this," he said at last.

Belle paused before speaking; she'd always been an optimistic person. "Isn't it possible this might be a prank, albeit a bizarre one? I haven't actually been threatened—"

"You were scared enough to leave your house, Belle."

"I know. But maybe we're overreacting—"

"Threats come in all sorts of guises. KIDNAPPED could be construed as one; so could DEATH TRAP and KILLER. My gut tells me we're dealing with a psychotic mind here, even if it is a prank. I mean, who frightens people just for the fun of it?"

Belle considered this. "Is there a possibility this puzzle could be tied to the crossword you brought me yesterday?"

Rosco thought. "That scenario would make me even more nervous than the idea of a loony-tune delivering a fake box of flowers."

Belle studied him, her brow wrinkled in thought.

"If there's a connection, Belle, it means someone's watching us . . . peeking in the windows . . . something like that. I bring you a puzzle Saturday afternoon. . . . We chat about it. . . . The next day, this wacko delivers his own weird offering—"

"I meant a link to yesterday's probable homicide."

"I don't follow you."

"You recognized similarities in the two deaths, Rosco: the newspapers under the bodies—"

"So you're suggesting that this hand-made puzzle is a follow-up to the printed crossword in the *Sentinel*?"

"I don't know," Belle said. "I admit the idea seems far-fetched. . . . For the timing to work, the cryptics editor at the Boston paper, Arthur Simon, would have to be cognizant of the scheme. . . ." She paused. "Forget the suggestion. I've met Arthur. He's a very straight arrow." Belle hesitated again.

"No, no, the same thought went through my mind yesterday when I bought the *Sentinel*. But after we completed the puzzle, I realized how far-fetched—"

"Wait! Let's return to your supposition—unpleasant as it is—that the person who delivered the flower box knew about yesterday's death, perhaps was even a witness, then saw you at the crime scene, saw you buy the *Sentinel*, recognized the newspaper, and created a puzzle with coded significance. . . . Some message we're not deciphering?"

Rosco pondered Belle's suggestion. "You don't happen to have the *Sentinel* crossword, do you?"

Belle's face brightened for the first time in many minutes. "Always be prepared," she said.

They laid the two cryptics side by side, looking for points of exchange; Belle even tried working the dual diagonals and reversing the puzzles and placing them head to foot. Nothing unconventional appeared. "I give up," she finally admitted, while Rosco shook his head.

"I'm thinking we should delay our wedding, if only for a week or two."

"Why?" Belle stared at him in bewilderment.

"If you're being targeted—and I strongly suspect you

are, given this flower box thing—it may not be wise to have a public ceremony. Psychos are psychos. I'd like to find this person before I let my guard down. Neither one of us needs to be distracted by this."

"It's not going to be public, Rosco. We'll be aboard the *Akbar*, and then, with any luck, at Cleo's. Besides, Al will be there the entire time." She forced a grim laugh. "Even in his groomsman togs I don't imagine he'd relinquish his official weapon."

Martha brought their meal, banging the plates down with a jovial: "This should wipe those sad-sack looks off your faces."

Belle and Rosco smiled reflexively, although the efforts were wan and lackluster. Neither began to eat.

"We can't postpone our wedding, Rosco. That's letting this weirdo win. And that's probably all he wants: to disrupt things, have a little private power play."

Again, Rosco was silent. Finally he said, "I want you to be careful. No opening the door to strangers. No walking along deserted streets. You need to be aware of who's nearby at all times. If this kook is aware of our marriage— and, again, given the florist's box and your recent notoriety—I'd say that was an excellent possibility, then the next six days could be critical. If he gets no reaction from this first puzzle, he'll move into some other phase of his plan. Who knows what it might be?"

Questions flooded Belle's brain, but each one was answered by the inevitable: If you achieve celebrity status— even as a minor-league celebrity—you become a target. "What do we do next?"

"I'm going to inform Al—"

She started to interrupt, but Rosco raised his hand in protest. "Lever believes you're the best thing that ever happened to me, Belle . . . something I'm inclined to agree with. He'll be as concerned as I am."

"I don't want a patrol car encamped on Captain's Walk, Rosco. That would look ridiculous."

Rosco thought. "And it might make the situation worse. Especially if this nut case believes he's scared you and decides to increase his fun. . . . Al will decide how he wants to handle surveillance."

Belle's expression turned grave. "Surveillance," she murmured.

"I'm going to start checking out florists this afternoon. And, to be perfectly honest, I'd be a lot happier if you'd consider moving in with Cleo or even Sara."

This time it was Belle who looked at the street. "I can't do that, Rosco. I'm too independent to be a house guest. I'll be fine at home. I promise."

"I could stay over. . . ."

"You'll have years of staying over come Saturday."

"You might change your mind after we get our license tomorrow."

Belle smiled and gave his hand a firm squeeze. "I'll be fine, Rosco. I will."

Martha reappeared. The hot smells of the kitchen followed her; it was a reassuring scent. "What's up with you two? Wedding jitters got you that bad?" She looked at the congealing food with thorough disapproval. "You can't put French toast in a doggie bag."

It was Rosco who answered. "We don't have a dog, Martha."

CHAPTER

13

The scent was so dense it made Rosco sneeze. Not once, but twice. He felt the reaction was almost uncouth in the rarefied atmosphere of tuberoses, anemones, lavender, lily of the valley, sprays of white lilac, boughs of blooming cherry and apple, and a profusion of other hothouse floral treasures. He sneezed again and retrieved a rumpled handkerchief. He was certain he was going to bash into some vase or other fragile receptacle and send it crashing to the floor. He sneezed a fourth and louder time.

"Gesundheit." The woman speaking had hair nearly as red as a satin Valentine's Day heart. She was outfitted in a form-fitting lime-green blouse and equally skintight pants. Rosco pegged her age at somewhere between forty and fifty, although he imagined she habitually admitted to being "in her thirties" and was actually in her sixties. "Flowers will do that to you. Me? I've been around them all my life. What can I do for you? No, let me guess: wife trouble."

Rosco looked too stunned to speak.

"I can pick 'em every time," the redhead continued. "Guys like you come into the shop. . . . They don't know their way around. . . . Never picked out a posy for the missus before. . . . But oops, they've found themselves in the doghouse, and they're barkin' to come home. Am I right?"

"Well, no," Rosco admitted. "I'm not married." But before he could add "almost, but not yet" to the statement, the redhead produced a low, voluptuous whistle.

"Really," she said. "A hunk like you. Go figure. I'm Faye. I'm the owner." Then, as if working on a weekend afternoon didn't suit her sense of her elevated status, she added. "Who else would be manning the fort on a Sunday? So, are we looking at a hospital visit, Mr.—?"

"Polycrates. Rosco Polycrates. I'm a private investigator."

Faye became a whirlwind of nervous energy. Her red-taloned fingers danced across the cash register; her hair shimmied on her jittery shoulders. "I swear I wasn't involved in anything that stupid kid did. I told the police that. The feds, too."

Rosco opened his mouth to speak, but her words barreled right past him.

"Look, you hire people because you think they're honest. Okay, okay . . . He had a cute bod; I'll admit it. But that's as far as it went. . . . When the bozo upped and disappeared, I was as surprised as everyone else. And, no, I haven't heard a word from him. That's the way it goes, isn't it? They take what they can and then light out. Unlucky in love, what can I say?"

When Faye finally began winding down, Rosco managed to speak. "I don't know anything about the 'bod,' the 'stupid kid,' the 'bozo.' I'm trying to hunt down an order that was delivered about midday."

Faye caught her breath and glared; the misunderstanding had severely shaken her. "You should have made that clear the minute you walked in here, mister," she spat out.

Rosco shrugged but didn't respond to her accusation. "A white box of long-stemmed roses? There was a scratch mark on one of the corners where a shop sticker might have been lifted off. Do you place stickers on your deliveries?"

"Sure, but those long-stem boxes come from a wholesaler in Lennox. Every shop in town gets them from the same place; probably half the people on the East Coast, too. I've sent out three long-stem orders so far today. What was the address?"

"Captain's Walk."

"Nope. Sorry."

"The box was tied with blue and cream-colored ribbon—"

Faye made a face. "What part of *nope* didn't you understand? The order didn't come from this shop. Nothing's been delivered to Captain's Walk in weeks. Besides, I'd never use those colors. They're dowdy. I like reds, fuschias, purple, American-beauty pink. But you're on the right track. Ya see, us florists use ribbons to identify ourselves. Call it our signature, because, when you think about it, there isn't a whole lot of difference between the flowers. . . . A rose is a rose, and all that malarkey. . . . Forget the box, concentrate on the ribbon. . . . No sticker and no greeting card, huh?"

"No. No business name or address," Rosco answered.

"Well, that's screwy right there. I'd never send anything out without my shop's name. How do you think I get return business? So what's going on? Someone trying to steal your honey from you? Mystery admirer?"

The thought that there might be some truth to Faye's question gave Rosco a slight chill. He shook it off with an uneasy smile and continued. "Do you have any idea which florist might use blue and cream-colored ribbons?"

"Do you have the ribbon?"

"In my car. I'll get it."

Rosco turned to leave, but Faye stopped him. "You might try Holbrook's," she said. "They're on Paine Boulevard, near Tenth Street. They've been around forever. Old Mr. Holbrook's ninety if he's a day. It sounds like the bland type of ribbon he might use. He does a lot of funerals. Were the roses red or yellow?"

"Those are my only choices?"

"Well, in long-stem, that's ninety percent of the business. Every now and then, white."

"The box was empty."

"Hah! Hah!" Faye laughed and rolled her eyes. "And that's what your honey-pie told you? You're in bigger trouble than you think, sweet pea."

It took Rosco only a few minutes to drive over to Holbrook's Florists. The shop itself was almost identical to Faye's in assortment of blooms and aromas. However, because the building was almost two hundred years older, there was a feeling of serenity and peace that was lacking in Faye's establishment. The ceiling was low, and the walls paneled with an antique mahogany that seemed to mimic the darkness of the South American jungle from which it had come. The fixtures were polished brass, and the cash register was antique, turn of the century, rather than a glowing computer screen. Clearly, Mr. Holbrook was accustomed to dealing with Newcastle's most affluent citizens, and Rosco found himself wondering how many times Sara Crane Briephs had patronized this particular business.

A small bell signaled his arrival, attracting the attention of the sales clerk, a man in his late thirties who reeked of Brooks Brothers: gray slacks and pale blue dress shirt whose French cuffs were adorned with conservative nautical-motif links. A navy blue bow tie and braces stitched from matching blue silk finished off the picture.

"Good afternoon, sir. Is there anything I can help you with today?"

The man's politeness was almost more than Rosco could stand. He produced the blue and cream-colored bow and said, "Yes, I was wondering if this ribbon might have come from your shop."

"Most definitely. In fact, I tied it myself."

"You seem awfully sure. You don't want to look at it a little more closely?"

"No. There's no need. It's Holbrook's ribbon. We special-order the line from Paris, and I recognize my own handiwork. It's from a long-stem rose order."

"I'm impressed," seemed to be all Rosco could think of saying.

"One's own artistry is often the easiest to recognize. May I ask to what this pertains?" The man glanced at his watch and then looked back at Rosco with the chagrined smile of a person who has just committed a grievous social error. "I apologize; we're due to close in five minutes. Sunday's hours are necessarily more abbreviated than weekdays. But please, I'm not trying to rush you."

"I'm a private investigator." Rosco handed the clerk a business card. "A floral box with this ribbon was delivered to a friend of mine earlier today. I'm trying to determine who sent it."

"We haven't delivered any long-stem orders today."

"You're sure?"

"Absolutely. And we surely would have included a card."

"But you tied the ribbon?"

The man took the ribbon from Rosco and looked at it more closely. After a moment, he said, "Yes, I definitely tied it. *When* I tied it, would be a much more difficult question to answer, however. You say it was delivered today?"

"Yep."

"Obviously not by us. What did the driver look like?"

"It was left on the porch."

"And you didn't see the truck, I take it?"

"Nope."

"Were the roses fresh? Maybe it's a delivery we made earlier this week, and the roses were recycled, if you will. It does happen, I'm sorry to say. Were they yellow or red?"

"There weren't any roses."

"What was in the box then, if I may ask?"

"Basically, it was empty."

The man appeared shocked. "And you believe Holbrook's would have forgotten to put the order into the box?"

Rosco placed the ribbon into his jacket and scratched his head. "No. I'm just trying to figure it all out."

"Well, Mr. . . ." The sales clerk looked at Rosco's business card; the corners of his lip curled downward in disdain. ". . . Polycrates, clearly someone found a discarded Holbrook's box and decided to play a practical joke on your friend. The ribbon is easily slid from the box and can just as easily be replaced."

"That would appear to be the case. How many long-stem orders have you had in the last week or so?"

The clerk strolled behind the counter and opened a small cedar filing box. The lid kept Rosco from observing the contents, but clearly the clerk was flipping through the delivery records. Eventually, he looked up at Rosco.

"We had six long-stem orders last week. All were deliveries. None picked up here at the shop."

"Could you tell me who they went to?"

"You must be joking!" He tapped the cedar box. "This is highly confidential information. I'm sure you can understand that not everyone who orders flowers, especially long-stem roses, is giving them to the person to whom they are wed."

"I see." Rosco glanced at his watch. "You close at three on Sundays, right?"

"Yes."

He gave the clerk a half smile. "Well, it's after three. How about I lock up for you?" He then walked to the front door, flipped the deadbolt, and turned back to face the clerk. "Now—"

"Sir, this is highly irregular," the clerk protested.

"More irregular than you might imagine. We need to conduct a little business here, and I think it's best if we weren't disturbed." Rosco reached for his wallet and placed two bills on the counter. "I'm in the market for something special for my fiancée, and I'm willing to spend two hundred dollars. Maybe you have what I'm looking for in the back room?"

The clerk stared at the money for nearly a minute before slipping it into his breast pocket and saying, "Let me see what I can find." He slid the cedar box toward Rosco and retreated through the shop's rear door. When he returned five minutes later, the box was open and Rosco was gone.

CHAPTER

14

Belle paced through her house. She was anxious and more than a little jumpy. Every noise seemed to portend danger; she imagined weird and conniving figures creeping near the windows to spy inside. *I've got to get a grip!* she silently warned herself. *Who'd be stupid enough to creep through the shrubbery on a gorgeous afternoon like this? Everyone on the block must be working in their gardens or painting shutters or something!*

Despite the pep talk, she continued stalking edgily through the rooms on the first floor. Completing a third tour, she stomped up the stairs, entered the bedroom, and barged into the bath that had been so exuberantly tiled in a black and white facsimile of a gigantic crossword puzzle. Belle shook her head irritably, sighed, tightened her lips in indignant anger at both herself and the situation, then returned to the steps, banging her feet on the treads as she descended. *I'm behaving like a cranky kid,* she thought, but the realization didn't diminish the uncomfortable sense of vulnerability nor Rosco's suggestion that someone had actually been spying on them.

She strode into her office and glared at the windows as if daring a pair of eyes to be peering back. "This is ridiculous!" she huffed aloud. "I'm not a coward. I won't be a prisoner in my own home."

With renewed determination, she marched toward the front door, grabbed the tan canvas jacket she kept on the coat rack, jerked open the door—and stopped cold. The street was stunningly empty, the neighboring gardens deserted, her own little patch of flowers and grass devoid of all life but birds and squirrels, insects and worms. *KIDNAPPED*, Belle remembered. If anyone intended to snatch her away in broad daylight, Captain's Walk on this astonishingly sleepy Sunday afternoon was the place to do it. Belle felt like whining in frustration.

She slammed the door shut, dumped her jacket on the floor, then slouched rebelliously back to her office. *KIDNAPPED*, she told herself as she whipped open her nearest English-language dictionary: *"To seize or detain or carry away by unlawful force or fraud and often with a demand for ransom." Ransom involves money,* Belle reasoned; *the victim is almost always a person of affluence which I, most definitely, am not.*

She closed the dictionary with a bang. *Could the crossword have been constructed as a different sort of warning?* she wondered. *Unlawful force or fraud.* Was it possible there was a hidden message beneath the most obvious references to blood and death? She unfolded the puzzle and began perusing it afresh. There was ROSCOE with an "e" at 8-Down, the clue naturally being a slang synonym for gun: a *Gat.* SEN was the solution to 12-Down: *Yen unit.* But SEN was often the abbreviation for senator, and Senator Hal Crane was Sara's well-heeled brother. Belle quickly dispensed with Rosco as a potential victim for the same reason she'd scoffed at considering herself. If a criminal wanted money, he—or she—would have to look elsewhere.

She stared at the letters again. *Roger* was the clue to 35-Down; RAY was the answer to 63-Down, ERMA at 66-Across. Belle sat back and thought for a moment. "Senator Crane," she finally muttered. The illustrious brother of Sara Crane Briephs, the man upon whose yacht Belle and Rosco would be wed.

She reached for the phone, intending to call Sara, although how she intended to broach the subject of a potential—and questionable—kidnapping of a U.S. senator, she wasn't certain, when the machine's loud ring made her jump. Belle grabbed the receiver from its cradle, almost shouting a nervous "Yes?"

"Is this Annabella Graham?"

"Speaking."

"My name is Elise Elliott. I'm a freelance journalist. I'm doing an article entitled 'Novel Nuptials' for the style section of the *Boston Sentinel*. The Sunday edition . . . ?"

Belle was silent. She stared at her office in confusion; a moment before she'd been pondering federal offenses; now she was being asked to chitchat about wedding preparations.

". . . I'm sorry to bother you on a Sunday afternoon, Miss Graham, but it's usually the best time to catch people at home. I wonder if I might ask you a few questions about your ceremony?"

"I . . . I have some important calls to make—"

"It won't take a moment, I assure you. The story concerns couples who've chosen innovative settings for their nuptials. I read in the article on you in *Personality* that you were planning a marriage ceremony at sea?"

Reluctantly, Belle began responding to the reporter's stock queries. "Yes, it's Senator Crane's boat, the *Akbar*," she said, spelling the word. "The yacht was named for the great Mogul emperor—"

But Elise Elliott wasn't interested in sixteenth-century India; instead, she interrupted with a cooing: "Will the senator be attending?"

Belle hesitated. Her brow wrinkled into a quick frown. SEN, she thought. Senator Hal Crane. "I'm not certain I should—" she began.

"Of course. Politicians are such busy, busy people, aren't they? Was this wedding at sea your idea or should we credit the husband-to-be?"

"Ummm . . . Actually, it was my idea. He sometimes has a problem with the water . . . a touch of *mal de mer*."

"That's often the best way to conquer your terror; just put yourself straight in the line of fire." Elise giggled, then immediately leapt to her next question: "Are you wearing a dress with a crossword design?"

"Pardon me?"

"In the *Personality* photo, your office is decorated with a word-game motif. I was wondering if you were continuing the black and white theme with your wedding attire."

"I . . . ah—"

The reporter stopped her with another tinkling laugh. "You wish to keep your gown a secret, I see. That's a wonderful touch! Traditionalists appeal to our readers. . . ." Belle heard the unmistakable sound of computer keys tapping out her response, but before she'd had a chance to object to this erroneous interpretation, Elise Elliott had moved on.

"I'm sorry for taking so long in getting your responses down, but this is a new notebook, and the computer commands are different from my old one. Ah . . . there . . . got it. . . . Now, would you mind sharing a quirky and intimate detail about your intended? I'm trying to keep a light and humorous feel to my story."

Without thinking, Belle blurted out, "He doesn't like wearing socks."

"Oh, my, that is intimate!" Again, the tinselly laugh. "No socks, but a gun . . . This *Roscoe* of yours must be quite a *pistol!*"

Belle opened her mouth to speak, but before she could do so, Elise Elliott had rung off with a cheery: "Thank you so very, very much, Miss Graham. I hope I won't need to trouble you again."

Belle stared at the phone for only a second before grabbing the receiver again. Her fingers jabbed the numbers for Boston-area information, which she followed immediately with a call to the *Sentinel*'s main switchboard. "Does an Elise Elliott write freelance articles for you?" Belle asked as soon as the newsroom desk answered.

The voice that responded was harassed, tired, and abrupt. "Who?"

"Her byline would be—"

"Call back Monday, sweetheart. I don't have time to hunt up every person who claims to write for this paper. If they don't have an extension and voice mail, I don't know them."

CHAPTER

15

The alley was almost pitch black, the buildings that lined it eerily quiescent. Only one of these structures appeared inhabited; it had a single lamp glowing within a second-floor window, but the light it sent down toward the potholed pavement below did nothing to alleviate the darkness. Adding to the sense of midnight desolation was a furtive scuffle of living creatures darting around the base of the buildings: rats climbing over metal garbage cans, the yowl of a stray cat. Then came the sound of human movement: whispers, a sudden cough, an oath from a voice that sounded younger and healthier than the first:

"Friggin' . . . ! That's gonna cost 'em! . . . New shoes . . . Just got them this morning, and I step into some friggin'—"

"Put a lid on it," the older man growled, then broke into another spasm of coughing.

"I'm not doing this anymore. I already tore my friggin' pants. It's ten times darker than Thursday, and you said—"

"Shut up. We do this and get out."

"Since when are you my boss?"

"Shut the hell up. You want the whole neighborhood to wake up?"

"What neighborhood?"

"Shut up, I said!"

"Nobody woke up Thursday, did they? And I mean, *nobody!*"

A distant siren screamed through the night; the speakers froze.

Finally, the younger man muttered an irate: "Our friggin' luck if that friggin' fire's in the next friggin' block."

"I told you to stuff it, already!" his companion shot back.

The noise drew closer, wailing a dissonant scream that then passed and grew rapidly fainter. The man with the cough resumed his tirade. "We grab the bricks; we do the job. Bing bang and we're outta here." He laughed with a bitter, hacking sound. "A lotta bang for the buck. This'll be the easiest hundred you ever made."

"Yeah? That's what you said Thursday, and look what happened. I nearly got mowed down."

"This ain't Thursday. I don't want to hear about Thursday."

"They're gonna pay for these shoes, though. Suede. You don't wash slop like this off suede. I laid out sixty bucks for these."

"I told you not to wear those stupid shoes," the older man answered, then added, "The bricks're over here. Just like the fella told us." He kicked at something that toppled with a solid thud onto the trash-strewn sidewalk. "A whole pile of these mothers."

"I got my gloves on me," the younger man boasted.

"You and your dainty hands!"

"Fingerprints, my man."

"On bricks? Fingerprints on bricks? You're stupider than I thought. If anything, the bricks're gonna leave marks on those dumb gloves. Then what happens when they catch up to you?" In the dim light, the cougher bent down and hefted a brick in his hand. "Every window," he barked. "Just like the man said."

"Every friggin' pane of glass," was the other's gleeful reply. He also bent toward the bricks, then swiftly stood, hurling his missile at the building lit with the solitary lamp. The older man immediately followed suit. Glass exploded into the empty air as brick followed brick, and window after window shattered.

Grunts of surprise and anger quickly began emanating from the building under attack. A second light came on, then another, and another. Someone started to moan in a high, keening pitch; someone began screaming obscenities.

The two stationed on the street heard a stern and commanding, "Okay, guys, calm down. Calm down! I'll handle this!"

"It's the friggin' priest," the younger man swore, but his companion had already dodged off down the alley.

Father Tom surveyed the damage. Nearly every ground-floor window had been broken, and many on the upper level, as well. Glittering shards of glass covered almost every surface, including the steps beneath the stairwell window. The kitchen was a disaster.

"They're trying to drive us out, for sure," one of the mission's eldest residents moaned.

"It's kids, Joe, just kids. Neighborhood punks," Father Tom answered. "No one's out to get us."

Another man took up the cry. Frightened, his speech became an indecipherable stutter. "Uh . . . uh . . . uh . . ." he mumbled.

Tom put a large and quieting hand on his shoulder. "It's okay, Clyde. You're okay. We're all okay. No broken bones. No cuts. No bruises."

But the priest's reassuring words were rapidly lost as individual residents began melding into one cowed and panic-filled body. Some of the less verbal men hissed; some rocked back and forth; all had nerves so overwrought the snap of glass crunching underfoot set them arguing ferociously.

"Shut your trap, Joe!" Tom heard.

"Why don't you shut yours?" another man viciously responded.

"You gonna make me?"

"Uh . . . uh . . ." Clyde continued while several of the others shouted a mocking: "Duh . . . duh . . . duh!"

Father Tom raised his arms. "Commend this food to our use, and us to your service. In Christ's name we pray."

It was an abbreviated form of the grace spoken at every meal, but they were words the residents of the Saint Augustine Mission instantly recognized and responded to. As if waiting to eat, all fell silent.

The priest allowed that calming spirit to swell through the frightened group. When he believed sufficient order had been reestablished, he spoke again. His tone was direct. He walked among the men as a general might walk among privates.

"Now, we've got some cleaning up to do. We'll organize ourselves into our regular work parties. First thing we want to do is get rid of this glass. Joe, let's get some brooms out here. Everything will be back to normal in no time. Clyde? You okay?"

Clyde stared but didn't attempt to speak. It was clear his moment of personal crisis was passing.

Another voice joined in. "You don't mind if I help out, do you, Padre?"

Father Tom turned. Standing by the open door, almost completely in shadow, was Gus Taylor. He was washed up, clean-shaven, and wearing freshly laundered clothes.

"Hello, Gus! Long time, no see." The priest's booming voice was full of approbation. All the mission residents looked up and grinned. One of their own returned, clean and sober; it was as if a saint had appeared in their midst. "Sure, Gus. We can use all the help we can get. Where've you been hiding yourself?"

"Well, you know how it is, Father, sometimes you bite the dog, sometimes the dog bites you."

Father Tom smiled in compassionate understanding. Gus Taylor might just make a comeback, after all. "Step inside and get some tea. I'm happy to see you're back on track. You didn't happen to see who did this, did you?"

"I saw a couple of guys hightail it down the alley when I was walking up here, but it was too dark to see their faces."

"Were they kids?"

"I don't think so. They were big. Maybe in their twenties." Gus approached Father Tom and lowered his voice. "I know you're trying to keep the peace here, Padre . . . especially with Clyde and Joe and some of the others being, well, a little, you know . . . but the guys who smashed your windows were goons. Hired hands, if you get my drift. Even if I'd been standing right in front of the mission when they started heaving bricks, I would have been afraid to step in."

Father Tom weighed this unwelcome news. "I intend to call the police. I don't think there's much they can do, but I'd like you to talk to them, tell them what you saw."

"I don't know any more than I just told you, Padre."

Fear had invaded Gus's voice. His hands began to tremble. Father Tom studied him for a moment. It wasn't unusual for the men at Saint Augustine's to be uneasy about the police department. Many had unsavory pasts, and often when a beat cop picked up a drunk in the street, it wasn't done with kid gloves. Still, Gus had once been a college professor and seemed to have no criminal record.

"Well, think about it. I won't ask you to do anything you don't want, but if someone's trying to put the mission out of business, I have no recourse but to fight."

"Like I said, Padre, it's darker than Hades out there—"

Father Tom silenced him with a sympathetic nod. "You do what you feel is best. Now, come on in and get some tea."

"Sure thing, Padre." Then Gus began to cough as if something in the air was catching.

CHAPTER

16

"That was relatively painless," Rosco said as he glanced at their freshly notarized marriage license. He and Belle had just stepped out onto the wide granite steps fronting City Hall. The sun was bright, and at nine-forty-five, the morning rush hour traffic had all but disappeared from Winthrop Drive. Belle smiled at him, leaned against one of the building's colossal Doric columns, and sighed with happiness. Her glow in the sunlight was impossible for Rosco to resist. He stepped toward her, and they exchanged a long and loving kiss.

"So far, this is the happiest day of my life," Belle finally said, "but Saturday will top it."

"No doubt about it."

"Assuming your sister's kitchen is finished."

"We'll survive, even if it isn't. Paper plates were invented for natural disasters such as this."

"You know what I love most about you, Rosco?"

"My snappy attire?"

"I'm being serious! What I most admire is—"

"My uncanny ability to find a parking place?"

"Rosco! I'm not making a joke! What I love about you is your optimism. It cheers me up just to be with you."

He held her again. "I wasn't always an always-look-on-the-bright-side guy, you know, but that changed when I met you. . . . In fact, I'd say that *you* were the one who makes me feel hopeful instead of the other way around."

She snuggled against him. "We're fortunate people, aren't we?"

"Yes, we are."

They walked slowly down the steps, the envelope containing the marriage license held tenderly in Rosco's hand. "You don't think that little snake of a bureaucrat will actually check the coordinates you gave her, do you?"

Belle's gray eyes sparkled with mirth. "Oh, I'm sure she will. But Captain Lancia swore up and down that's exactly where the *Akbar* will be the moment we're married: latitude forty-one degrees, fifty-six minutes, north, longitude seventy degrees, fifty-one minutes, east. I have it committed to memory. It's right out there in Buzzards Bay. I checked it in my atlas just to be sure."

"I knew there was another reason I loved you." Rosco gave Belle a third kiss.

"Hey, hey, you two, break it up." Al Lever trudged toward them as he spoke. "We'll have no public displays of affection around here. This is city property."

"Spoken like a true civil servant."

"I thought I'd find you here. How'd it go with Miss Sharpened Pencil in there?"

Rosco waved the license.

"Finished already? That's got to be record time. Congratulations are in order."

"Save it for Saturday," Rosco said, grinning at Belle. "When it's official."

"I'm only congratulating you on securing the license, Polly—crates. One step at a time. But speaking of official, how'd you like to do a little *un*official work. Pro bono, actually . . ."

"Al," Belle protested, "we're getting married in five days. Don't you think you should leave him alone?" She hooked her arm in Rosco's.

Lever smiled, although he didn't acknowledge Belle's objection. "Did you ever find that dog you were looking for, Polly—crates? Freddie Carson's dog?"

"That problem's been put on the back burner. Something a little more pressing came up."

"Oh yeah?"

Rosco and Belle shared a glance. She nodded her head in silent agreement.

"Someone delivered a crossword to Belle's house yesterday. A bunch of unpleasant clues and answers . . . in a box intended for long-stem roses, no less. I'd like to find out who it was."

Lever's brow creased. "Sounds to me like some loony practical joker, or are you thinking it's an actual threat?"

"I feel it should be viewed as a threat until I can prove otherwise."

"That's the problem with fame," Lever said. "Every weirdo in the world wants in on the act. . . . You want a patrol car up on Captain's Walk, Belle? Just till the wedding?"

"I'm all right, Al. I don't want the neighbors going nuts on me."

"It wouldn't be a problem to supply a little additional protection."

"I'm fine, Al, really."

"She's a stubborn woman." Rosco squeezed Belle's hand. "I started checking out the situation yesterday afternoon. I gather NPD had already had dealings with the first florist I questioned . . . a redhead named Faye. . . ."

Rosco continued detailing his preliminary investigation, then concluded with: "Four of the long-stem boxes had been delivered to private homes. I made inquiries. Dead end each time; they still had the empty boxes in their trash. The other two deliveries went to commercial addresses. That's where I'm headed now."

Lever pulled a pack of cigarettes from his breast pocket, lit one, then squinted through the smoke. "A couple of lowlifes smashed the windows in the Saint Augustine Mission last night. Did you hear about that?"

It was Belle who answered, her face suddenly drawn and worried. "You're kidding! What about Margaret House?"

"The nuns weren't hit. . . . Just Father Tom's place."

"I usually volunteer at the women's shelter Monday mornings," Belle said. Her voice was quiet.

"Like I said, the vandalism was confined to the men's mission, although—"

"Although?" Belle interrupted.

Lever's response was thoughtful. "I gather something—or someone—scared off the thugs. Otherwise, who knows? Maybe they were intending on hitting the women's home, as well."

Rosco shook his head. "Two potential homicides, this vandalism, and all directed at . . ." He paused and studied his former partner's face. "Did you ever get an ID on the woman over at the bus depot?"

"Not yet. But it turns out the mud on her boots wasn't

from around here. Jones is trying to place it, but hell, she could've been from anywhere—"

It was Belle who interrupted. "Are you thinking that the Peterman brothers are involved in some fashion, Al?"

Lever looked at Rosco; Rosco turned to Belle, who then refocused her attention on Al. "Let me clarify that question. We are discussing an unofficial comment, aren't we?"

"With a great big *U*. And you didn't hear it from me. Like they say: You don't buck City Hall . . . or friends of friends on the City Council. But let's take a look at who stands to make out big time when this empowerment zone goes through. And believe me, it *will* pass City Council."

Rosco took Belle's hand, a feeling of tacit agreement passed between them. "What do you want from us, Al?" Belle asked.

"From you, nothing. From the blushing groom there . . . a little pro bono work for Father Tom. The detective assigned to the shelter problem is booked to the gills with priority cases, which may not be such a bad situation. Ever notice how quiet people get when police ask questions?"

"You want me to find the goons who broke the windows?"

Lever nodded. "According to your friend Gus Taylor, it was a couple of low-rent hoods—"

"How did he—?"

"I'll fill you in later," Lever answered. "*After* you agree to help out . . . *unofficially*. I know the timing's rotten, but if we can link these guys to—"

Rosco didn't need to look at Belle to gauge her reaction. "I just might be able get a line on these goons, Al. There's a guy who owes me a little something. But I've got another couple of phantom flower deliveries to track down, okay? Then I'm all yours."

Belle squeezed his hand.

"Until Saturday, that is."

Lever crushed his cigarette out on the City Hall steps. "Just get me a couple of names; NPD'll take it from there. Stop by my office. I'll give you all the pertinent information."

Belle and Rosco watched the detective trot down the steps to his brown sedan.

"Thanks," she finally said. "For helping Father Tom, I mean."

"I want to do this, Belle. For myself as well as for you and Tom." He pulled her close and kissed her again. "Dinner tonight?"

Belle nodded, then looked into his eyes. "You'll call me this afternoon?"

"You bet."

"Be careful."

"Careful's my middle name."

"I mean it, Rosco. Guys who are hired to smash windows aren't all that pleasant."

Rosco knew there was no guarantee that either one of the remaining long-stem rose boxes was the one that had been delivered to Belle's porch. But he was also aware that it was the only lead he had. His search the previous evening had been spectacularly unsuccessful. The clerk at Holbrook's had been correct: Giving flowers was deeply personal. "None of your damn business" had been the most popular reply to his question: "Did you receive any roses recently?" But the mention of Belle's name and the fact that she'd been the target of a malicious hoax had elicited more positive responses . . . another indication of celebrity's allure.

With four orders accounted for, Rosco now found himself standing at the corner of Eleventh and Hawthorne, hot on the trail of the fifth gift box. It seemed ironic that the *Evening Crier* building sat on the southeast corner of the intersection. Kitty-corner there was a men's clothing store. The other two corners sported banking institutions. It was the Second National Bank, and a Mr. Clover in particular, who had received the roses from Holbrook's.

"I'm looking for Mr. Clover," Rosco said to the security officer as he exited the bank's revolving door.

The guard pointed. "That's him at the third desk . . . in the gray suit."

"Thank you."

Rosco approached Clover's desk and removed a business card from his jacket. Since the brush-with-celebrity approach seemed to work the night before, he opted to try it again, "Excuse me, Mr. Clover?"

"Yes."

"My name is Rosco Polycrates. I'm a private investigator. I'm working for Belle Graham."

Clover's chuckle threw Rosco off guard.

"According to what I read in *Personality* magazine, you're *marrying* Belle Graham. I hope you're not considering it *work* already?"

Rosco considered a witty rejoinder but had none. "Do you mind if I sit?"

"Please do." Clover stood and extended his hand. "Call me Carl. I'm a big devotee of your fiancée's puzzles. I don't miss a day."

"Thank you. She'll be happy to hear she has a fan across the street."

"Indeed. I've got a wonderful view of the *Crier* building

from my desk here. I don't see much of Miss Graham though."

"You know what she looks like, then?"

"She's hard to miss. Quite a beautiful young lady, if you don't mind me saying so. There's a lot of men in Newcastle who consider you a very lucky fellow."

Rosco hesitated. "The reason I'm here is because I believe you ordered a dozen long-stem roses from Holbrook's last week."

Again, Clover chuckled. "It was my aunt who ordered them. For my birthday. My fifty-fifth. She's a bit of an oddball, and unfortunately, never remembers that I'm violently allergic to roses. We go through the same routine every year, and every year, I have to surreptitiously dispose of her gift."

"You threw the flowers away?"

"No. I gave them to a couple on the street after I finished work. They seemed very happy."

Rosco glanced at his notepad. "And this was Friday evening?"

"Yes. The bank stays open till nine P.M. on Fridays. It was almost ten when I left."

"Did you know the people?"

"No."

"Would you recognize them again? Were they old? Young?"

"Very young. Eighteen or so. My offering made quite an impression, and, by coincidence, gave me a wonderfully unexpected birthday present. The young lady opened the box, scooped up the roses, put one between her teeth and danced across the sidewalk—"

"And the box?"

"What about it?"

"What'd they do with it?"

Clover smiled indulgently. "They dropped it. Right at their feet. They were very young and very happy. I tidied up after them. Why do you ask?"

"A long-stem rose box was left on Belle's porch yesterday. I'm trying to determine where it came from."

Clover looked out the window and pointed across the street. "Do you see the phone booth beside the *Crier* building? There's a trash container on the far side. I deposited the box there. I would have brought it back to the bank, but the building was locked by then." He thought for a moment. "And now that you mention it, I don't remember noticing the box when I returned for work on Saturday morning."

"Really? That trash can's kind of hard to see from here."

Clover's voice cracked slightly. "Oh, I park in the *Crier* lot, so I pass the receptacle each morning."

"Ever make any telephone calls from that booth over there?"

"Why would I do that? I have a phone right here on my desk."

"Just curious."

Rosco reentered the street. As Clover had indicated, the trash container was beside the phone booth, the booth from which the anonymous call about the dead woman had originated. As he headed toward his Jeep, Rosco began running a number of seemingly unrelated facts through his brain:

A crossword that spelled DEATH TRAP, a pair of probable homicides, two hired goons, and a floral box missing its roses. *Coincidence,* he thought. That was the word Clover had used, but Rosco had never put much faith in the concept.

As he set out to interview the recipient of the sixth order of roses, a dress shop on Ninth Street, he had a strong hunch he'd already found what he was looking for, and there was nothing *coincidental* about it.

CHAPTER

17

"What a mess you've made!" The voice was gravelly and gruff, any inherent kindliness muted by fatigue and fear. "You gotta go outside to do your business! I told you that before I left. That's how come there's a hatch in the door over there."

A whimper greeted the words, followed by the sound of four small paws treading on soaked and scattered newspaper. A single light fixture dangling on a long, brown cord swayed slightly, throwing a harsh reflection at the greasy window and the black night beyond. Aside from the light, the room was furnished only with a sink, a chair, and a square table that looked none too clean.

"Peeughh . . . It surely does stink in here. Lucky thing we don't have to worry about neighbors." There was a laugh here, a bray of brief bravado. "That nice middle-class ideal: neighbors, kids playing outdoors, washing machines, bikes on every porch, dogs underfoot." The cynical tone devolved into one of vitriol. "What am I gonna do with a damn dog?"

Sensing danger, little Kit Carson made no sound.

"A damn dog! And here, of all places! I've always been too friggin' soft-hearted. A dog! Who knew that bum had a dog with him? And a puppy, no less. A full-grown stray I could have left. It would have taken care of itself, just like all the others slinking around the damn city. But a pup, that's what I got! A friggin' puppy!"

Kit whined and flattened herself on the sodden paper.

"Shut up, you! I gave you food, didn't I? Water . . . a roof over your head . . . And what have you done? Made a pigsty of my place!"

Tired hands reached down and began cleaning up the mess. "You trash your fresh water like you did these newspapers, you'll have nothing to drink. I'm not your damn nursemaid. I'm not gonna spoon-feed you. Give you sips of sweet water. You don't eat and drink, you die. That's the law of nature. Survival of the fittest." The tough talk was now etched with panic.

"If I'd known that stupid guy had a dog . . . !"

The chore of picking up after the puppy continued. The sounds were loud and aggressive: the clump of boots, the crash of chipped bowls that had contained food and water.

"You ate all the canned stuff, I see. Learned expensive tastes from your loving master. . . . No cereal and filler for her highness, here." Water was sloshed into a bowl; a can was opened and its contents plopped into another, then both containers were slammed back on the floor.

"If that damn woman hadn't come after me like she did . . ." The voice mimicked a high-pitched whine. " 'I'll call the authorities!' she tells me. 'I'll have you evicted!'

The bitch had it coming, didn't she? She friggin' had it coming!"

Instead of approaching her food, Kit crept under the table. "You're damn right to keep out of my way! If it hadn't been for your damn owner, I'd be sitting in clover right now." A near sob broke through the tirade. "What am I gonna do with a friggin' dog? I can kill a person. I can't snuff a friggin' puppy. I have to make some adjustments here."

CHAPTER

18

Tuesday morning arrived with "a mixture of clouds and sunshine," just as the weatherman had predicted. Belle took her mug, with its treasured dregs of stone-cold coffee, and wandered into her home office. The nervousness she'd experienced with the delivery of Sunday's unsettling crossword was beginning to fade. That was the good news.

The bad news was that Rosco had failed to beam in with an update, let alone give her a late-night sleep-tight call. Her assumption had been that he'd arrived at his apartment at some hideous hour and had deemed it much too late to phone her. That same regard for an uninterrupted night's sleep was what filled Belle's own head at this moment. Seven-twenty A.M. was far too early to call anyone, especially if that anyone hadn't gone to bed before three or four in the morning. These thoughts only served to focus Belle on her wedding: a day that would signal the beginning of life as part of a couple, a day when Rosco's often problematic schedule would produce even greater apprehension, because he'd be arriving home to her.

Belle set her coffee mug on her work desk, dropped herself into a black and white canvas deck chair, let out a long sigh, then glued her eyes to the telephone. "Maybe, if I stare at it long enough, he'll wake up and give me a call. . . ."

After another thirty seconds, the phone rang. She jumped in her seat and grabbed the receiver. "If I'd known it would be that easy, I would have pulled this trick an hour ago. What did you learn?"

"P-p-pardon me?"

Although the voice seemed shaky, Belle easily recognized it as Rosco's sister Cleo.

"Cleo?"

"Belle, hi . . . um . . . *Listen,* is Rosco there?" The tension in her tone was palpable.

"No, he's at his apartment . . . Are you all right?"

"I *called* his *apartment,* his *office* . . . and his car phone. There's *no* response *anywhere.*"

Belle's initial reaction was bewilderment. Where was Rosco? But the larger issue was his sister's obviously urgent need to find him.

"Is there anything I can help you with, Cleo?"

Cleo remained silent for an uncomfortable minute. When she spoke, her tone was a staccato burst, interspersed with anxious and irate sighs. "Somebody just *phoned* here. . . . I don't know why my husband's *always* out of town when these *creepy* things happen. He drives me *crazy* sometimes—"

"Who called? What was it in reference to?"

"Some *man* . . . About ten minutes ago. Actually it *could* have even been a woman, now that I *think* about it. The voice was really *odd.*"

"What did this person want, Cleo?"

"He said he was going to call *back.*"

"That's it?"

"No, no . . . *First* he asked how the *wedding* plans were coming along. It was *really* bizarre. I mean at seven-something in the morning? Who's thinking about a *wedding?* I was getting Nicky ready for school . . . Effie's got a *cold* or something . . . so I was *wide* awake. Then he asked to talk to *Rosco.*"

"Rosco?"

"I told the guy to wait until *nine* o'clock and call Rosco's office, but he said he'd *already* tried his office, home, and car phone. So, I told him to call *you.* He said Rosco wasn't *there* either. Did this guy contact you, Belle?"

"No."

"Then how'd he know Rosco wasn't *there?*"

"I don't know. I don't know." Belle began to pace her office, the long telephone cord following her like a pet snake.

"I tried *all* of Rosco's numbers after he'd hung up," Cleo continued, "but there was *no* answer. . . ."

Belle thought for a moment. "And that was the extent of your conversation?"

"No. . . . After telling me he'd call back, the guy said, 'Rosco's missing in action,' just like that. Real *deadpan.* It was *impossible* to tell if it was a *question* or a *statement.* I asked what he *meant,* but the line went dead. I *hate* it when my husband goes out of town like this. . . . It's as if someone's *watching* to see when he *leaves* the house."

Belle took a deep breath. "Listen, Cleo, I'm going to drive by Rosco's apartment and office. . . . Then I'm coming over to your house. I want to be there when this person calls again, okay? It shouldn't take me much more than an hour."

"*Thanks,* Belle. I'll get someone to take Nicky to school so I don't miss you. I won't ask you to *hurry,* but . . ."

It was Effie who opened the door. The five-year-old was not attired as a ballerina this time; instead, she'd draped herself in a collection of oversized garments obviously borrowed from her mother. The cold that was keeping her home from school didn't seem to be affecting her sense of style. "I'm a princess," she said, eyeing Belle with her customary mixture of mistrust, jealousy, and fascination. "Are you wearing a white dress and a veil on Saturday?"

"No, I'm not, Effie."

"Why not? Aren't you supposed to be a bride?"

The subject of remarriage and glowing white felt too complex for a pint-sized princess. "Is your mom around?" Belle said in an attempt to change the subject. "I told her I'd come over—"

"Mommy does the same thing when she won't tell me something," Effie announced coolly, then added an equally unemotional "She's at the vet's. Geoffrey's baby-sitting, 'cause I'm too sick to go to school." The cabinetmaker's name was pronounced with a regal flourish as if her highness was considering a knighthood for Geoffrey Wright.

"But . . ." Belle began, but Effie had already raced off in a trail of multicolored silk.

Belle heard a squeal, a crash that sounded like a door slamming hard, and a shout of "Give it back, you stupid dog!" She left the house and entered the garage.

"Hiya, Tinker Bell," was Geoff's brief greeting, then his

focus immediately returned to the wood panel he was laboring over. A can of cherry-colored stain sat on the workbench beside him, as well as a variety of sandpapers, wads of steel wool, and a selection of paintbrushes. "Good news," he added without looking up. "I talked to Sharon last night. She's on her way down from Vermont this afternoon. Even if the dishwasher doesn't arrive, she and I can hang some of the cabinets—"

Belle interrupted with a hurried, "Effie said her mom's gone to the vet's?"

"Emergency with one of the dogs . . . the basset, I think. She told me to tell you—"

"We spoke an hour ago; there was no mention of a problem with a dog." *Missing in action,* Belle thought, *Rosco's missing in action.* Tension made her throat tight, and her tone high-pitched and edgy.

Geoffrey glanced up briefly. "Hey, Tinker Bell, relax! You're a pretty lady. I hate to see you get so—"

"Cleo called me . . . She said I should hurry. . . ."

"What can I say? Emergencies happen." Geoff lightly brushed the cabinet's surface with steel wool while Belle frowned in confusion.

"What happened to the dog?" she said at last.

"Ate something nasty, I suppose. Cleo came out here to talk to me and found the basset on the lawn out there, curled up in a ball and crying. She assumed it had been poisoned on account of it's barking all the time and driving the neighbors bonkers. You know how Cleo is; likes the dramatic. . . . But I think the pooch got into a garbage can somewhere. Bassets will gorge on anything and *everything,* you know."

Belle's frown increased. Something about the recitation sounded wrong, but she wasn't sure where the problem lay.

"I'm surprised you didn't notice the dog was ill before Cleo did."

"When I've got that electric sander revved up, I wouldn't hear a military helicopter landing in the driveway."

"And you've no idea when Cleo's expected to return?"

"Not a clue—"

"Or the name of the animal hospital?"

Geoffrey Wright looked at her, his expression suddenly stony. "I'm a cabinetmaker, Belle. I'm working in this house as a craftsman, not a chamber maid . . . or a babysitter."

Belle's face grew hot; she was about to respond when the phone rang.

Geoff picked up the receiver, cradling it against his neck while both hands continued to work. "It's for you," he said.

"But nobody—" Belle began as she reached for the phone. "Belle Graham speaking."

The voice was not as mechanical as an automated directory assistance announcement, but it was eerily devoid of expression. ". . . on the dashboard," it insisted.

"Hello?" Belle answered. "Hello?"

". . . quotation," the voice added. "Our little secret . . . I think you'll like it."

"Who is this? Where's Rosco?" Belle demanded, but the reply was an impassive:

"One hour . . . Identify the quotation, if you dare." There was a firm click on the other end of the line.

Belle replaced the receiver and unconsciously looked at her watch. It was eight-forty-five.

"Bad news?" Geoff asked the question as he dipped a brush into the can of wood stain. He couldn't have seemed less concerned.

"Just a crank call. I get them on occasion."

"I'm surprised someone phoned you here," was his blasé observation. "Your own home, sure. But not your future sister-in-law's place."

"The price of fame." Belle's laugh was thin and forced. "No one's safe." She walked toward the garage's open doors. "I'm going to step outside for a minute."

Geoffrey was so intent on applying the stain that he didn't realize Belle was gone when he said, "You should move to Vermont. Forget the celebrity bit . . ."

Belle sauntered across the drive, pretended to stretch, then walked toward her car. The crossword puzzle wasn't on the dashboard as the caller had promised. Instead, it lay upside down on the driver's seat. Belle glanced back at the garage, then reached for the hand-drawn cryptic. Across its top were crude block letters inked in heavy black: "Not Dreaming."

Across

1. Groom without an E?
6. Butts
10. "The———of War"
14. Mr. Chekhov
15. Theater org.
16. Opera solo
17. Chars
18. Stratagem
19. Drug fed
20. "Can we———?"
21. Certain strangler
22. "Each man———the thing he loves," Wilde
23. Quote, part 1
27. 67-Across, e.g.
28. Old Rough and Ready
31. Quote, part 2
34. Part of A&P
35. Jazz job
37. March 15th, e.g.
38. Quote, part 3
40. Opera d'———
41. First lady
42. Shoe size
43. Quote, part 4
45. Demand
48. Took a dip
49. Quote, part 5
54. Where Macbeth kills Duncan
57. Purchase
58. To be in Paris
59. Kidnapper's payoff, slang
60. Mil. branch
62. Show the way
63. Mil. branch
64. Check out the web
65. Actress Sharon
66. Classic Altman film
67. Stack part
68. Aides

Down

1. Selassie worshiper
2. Hoopster Shaq
3. "———for time"
4. Source of a bottleneck stopper
5. Switch positions
6. "In Cold Blood" author
7. Husband's sister
8. Bygone Pontiac
9. "Do as I———"
10. Mr. Webster
11. Spoken
12. "My———," Temptations' hit
13. Certain plant parts
21. Most pleasant
22. "The Glass———"
24. Garden tool
25. "———Brute?"
26. Hoard
29. Monster
30. John & Paul's meter maid
31. "———on a Grecian Urn"
32. Sitarist Shankar
33. British gun
34. Lincoln or Burrows
36. Diamond, e.g.
39. Son of 41-Across
40. 4-doors have 4
44. Pop
46. Bait &———
47. Certain Richard
48. Murders
50. Some supports
51. Beliefs
52. Ain't right?
53. Ponds, across the Pond

NOT DREAMING

54. **Astringent**
55. ————**Nostra**
56. **Sever & Smothers**
60. **Mil. branch**
61. **Take to court**
62. **Mil. branch**

CHAPTER

19

ROSCO. Sitting alone in Cleo's second-floor guest bedroom, Belle stared at the letters she'd just added to the crossword grid. 1-Across: *Groom without an E?*

"ROSCO," she said aloud. "ROSCO." Her spine tingled in fear. Who was this mystery constructor, and what did he—or she—want? Belle glanced at her watch; "One hour," the peculiar voice had ordered. "Identify the quotation, if you dare."

She returned to the crossword, carefully filling in solutions with her red pen. PLOY was the answer to 18-Across; KILLS was at 22-Across: *"Each man KILLS the thing he loves"*—an adage from Oscar Wilde.

"ROSCO," she repeated aloud. Could it be that he'd been the target all along? Had the florist's box been a ruse, and the hand-made puzzle she'd received Sunday merely a means to bring him in contact with a killer?

Belle tried to sort through the chain of events: A one-time resident of the Saint Augustine Mission had been murdered, then a nameless woman found dead near the bus depot. Father Tom's shelter had been vandalized, after which had come a sinister cryptic in an empty flower box, a peculiar call to Cleo stating that Rosco was "missing in action," and now another cryptic.

"Each man KILLS the thing he loves." Belle repeated aloud as she picked up the telephone and punched in the number of Rosco's mobile unit, hoping against hope that he would finally answer. At the same moment, Effie barged into the room.

"Whatcha doing?"

"Calling Uncle Rosco."

"Why?"

Belle plastered on a falsely sanguine smile. "Because I haven't talked to him in a while."

Rosco's phone rang and rang. He was obviously not in his car. Belle redialed his office, but with no success. The answering machine picked up immediately, indicating there were a stack of messages. She added another to the list.

"Maybe he doesn't want to be found," Effie suggested calmly. "Like my dad. My mom says hiding is Daddy's favorite thing. I think he's hiding now. That's why he's not here."

Belle gazed at the little girl, but no further family secrets were forthcoming. Instead, Effie waltzed off, bossily scolding one of the dogs as she meandered through the upstairs hall. Belle glanced at her watch. Nineteen minutes were left in the hour she'd been allotted.

A quote in five parts, she told herself as her pen raced over the paper. NARC, she wrote at 19-Across; SNUFFS was the solution to 48-Down: *Murders.* 55-Down was COSA *Nostra.* Belle felt her skin prickle; her forehead was damp; her palms wet. PLOY, she wrote. KILLS.

Cleo returned home, yelling for Effie, and the decibel level in the house increased one hundredfold. "Belle, *honey bunch*," she called up the stairs. "Sorry I had to *rush* out, and leave you *hanging*. I'll fill you in in a minute."

Effie spoke before Belle had a chance to reply. "She tried to call Uncle Rosco. He's hiding just like Daddy does."

Belle heard Cleo laugh uneasily; her voice grew more boisterous in compensation. "I'll make us some *coffee*. At least I can still heat *water* in that mess of a *kitchen!*" Then she was gone amid yips, yelps, bursts of "Mom!" "Mommy!" and her own clamorous responses.

Belle looked at her watch. Twelve minutes remained. *"Quote, part 1,"* she muttered. *"Quote, part 2,3,4, and 5."* Her pen scribbled furiously; she gnawed her lip in concentration. Finally, she gasped and sat very still.

"ALL THAT WE SEE OR SEEM IS BUT A DREAM WITHIN A DREAM." They were lines from an Edgar Allan Poe poem. She stared at the cryptic's title, "Not Dreaming," suddenly recalling other lines. As she did, an eerie suspicion crept over her. Was it possible that the person who'd constructed the crossword was aware of her love of poetry? Or was this merely coincidence?

"O, God! can I not save/One from the pitiless wave?" she recited silently. "ALL THAT WE SEE OR SEEM/IS BUT A DREAM WITHIN A DREAM." *Pitiless wave,* she thought, then added a wary, *Rosco!*

Belle stood; in six short minutes, the hour would be up. She hurried downstairs, where Cleo met her, carrying two mugs brimful of syrup-thick Greek coffee. The two women almost collided.

"Any word from your fellow?" Cleo's face bore a taut and worried expression.

"Nothing."

Cleo studied Belle. "Geoffrey said you had a phone call . . . *here*. . . . Someone contacted you here."

"A crank call. I get them on occasion."

Belle assumed a nonchalant attitude as she put her coffee mug on a table, then surreptitiously folded the crossword into ever smaller pieces. "Our secret," the mystery caller had warned; and until she knew more, there was no point in causing Cleo further alarm. "Is the basset hound okay?"

Cleo sipped at her coffee, but her thoughts were clearly far from the ailing dog. "Oh, sure. Buster ate something that made him sick. A big fuss for *nothing*. Why would *you* get a phone call at *my* house?"

Belle skirted the question, instead saying, "Rosco's a private investigator, Cleo. Before that, he was a cop. You know his schedule's not an easy one and that he can't always check in—"

" *'Missing in action'* is what the weirdo said."

Belle put her hand on her future sister-in-law's shoulder. "There are a lot of kooks out there . . . folks who get their jollies from placing obscene or harassing phone calls . . . and with the wedding so near . . ." Belle affixed a hopeful grin. "Did Geoff tell you Sharon is on her way back?"

Cleo ignored the information. "But why does this *sicko* call *now?* When there's no *man* in the house! This thing has given me the *willies!*"

"Geoffrey's here," Belle offered while Effie, who had crept close, added an enthusiastic: "And Sharon! She's strong! She's coming back!"

Cleo snorted angrily. "I got *kids*. I don't want a *nut case* prowling around!" Then she spun on her daughter with an abrupt: "Effie, take that stuff off *now!* You *can't* eat lunch in that *dopey* getup."

The princess burst into tears; Belle found herself consoling her petite rival and murmuring soothing phrases of encouragement. The child's unhappy snuffles changed to wounded pride. "Aunt Belle likes my costume, don't you Aunt Belle?" Gone in the twinkling of an eye was the odious Tinker Bell; Belle had been promoted to Aunt.

She beamed in gratitude. "I think you look just like a queen—"

At that moment, the phone rang. Both women jumped; the healthy dog started barking ferociously; Effie noisily shushed it while and Cleo and Belle simultaneously grabbed for the receiver. Cleo won.

"Yeah? . . . What? . . . I'm having a hard time hearing you. . . . Effie, be *quiet* for a second, *will* ya . . . Hello . . . *Hello?*" She handed the cordless to Belle; beneath her pancake makeup, her blue eye shadow, and outlined lips, her skin was gray. "Guy for you. . . . Talks like a stupid *answering machine.*"

Belle took the phone, pressed it hard against her ear, and walked from the room, but the familial noise pursued her. "Get *back* here, Effie! No, *Buster's* gotta stay outside."

"Hello?" Belle said; she could feel her breaths growing shallow and nervous.

" 'A DREAM WITHIN A DREAM': I hope you were suitably impressed, Belle. I may call you, Belle, may I not?"

"Who is this?"

"Someone who'd like to get to know you better. It sounds as if you are in the midst of a most delightful gathering. Family life is gratifying, isn't it?"

"Who is this?" Belle repeated. She avoided looking back at Cleo.

"I think we'll keep that another secret for the time being. . . . You haven't told anyone about our little game, have you?"

"No . . . I haven't told anyone."

"Except Rosco."

"Pardon?" Belle's heart felt as if it had stopped.

"You shared my first missive with your paramour. Silly girl . . . Don't you know what we're doing here?"

"No . . . no, I don't. . . ."

"We're building a working relationship, dear heart."

The line went dead, then immediately rang a second time.

"Yes?" Belle almost shouted into the receiver.

"Hey, Hey! Tinks!" she heard. "You don't need to bite my head off. It's Geoff. . . . I'm on the cellular. Tell her regalness I'm heading downtown to the hardware store. Anything she needs, have her beep me. . . . Oh, Sharon beamed in a couple of minutes ago. Her ride's on the fritz. She's catching a bus and will call from the depot." Then that connection also ended.

Belle stared at the now quiet machine. Punching in the code to retrieve the last caller's ID would only reveal Geoff's car phone. The mystery crossword constructor's number had been obliterated.

CHAPTER

20

Abe Jones drummed the fingers of his right hand on the pink Formica countertop, while he rolled a packet of Sweet'n Low through the fingers of his left. The move resembled a Mississippi River gambler manipulating a weatherbeaten ace of hearts. The packet appeared and disappeared: pink paper fluttering briefly in the air. Abe watched his fingers work, then stared pensively across the coffee shop.

At twelve-fifteen, Lawson's was a madhouse. The lunch-hour rush was in full swing. Waitresses flew by, laden with armloads of sandwich platters and fried fish entrées, alternately shouting harried greetings to regular customers and orders for additional chips and extra mayo to Kenny, the short-order cook. Jones took it all in, while remaining silent and seemingly unaffected.

He dropped the sweetener packet back into a chrome bowl as Al Lever slid his beefy frame onto the stool beside him. "Sorry I'm late. . . . Thought I'd walk over; get some exercise. . . . I'll never try a crazy stunt like that again." He looked around the coffee shop. "This place is a zoo. I was hoping we could get a booth."

"We've got a better chance of winning the lottery."

"Coffee, doll?" It wasn't Martha, but a Martha-in-training who interrupted.

"Thanks, Lorraine." Lever looked at Jones. "Did you order yet?"

Jones shook his head. "I was waiting for you." He looked at Lorraine and smiled his signature grin. "How about a pastrami on rye?"

"You bet, sugar. What about you, doll?"

"BLT . . . white toast . . . extra mayo on the side."

Lorraine cocked a skeptical eyebrow as she jotted the order onto a pad; then she turned, pushed the slip of paper through the pickup window, and shouted, "Two live ones, Kenny. Extra mayo for big Al, here."

Lever ignored the jibe and focused on Jones. "So, what have we got?"

Abe pulled a small spiral notebook from his breast pocket and flipped it open. "Let's start with the first one: Freddie Carson and Adams Alley. It's fairly simple; Carlyle places the time of death at three-thirty or four in the morning. Our weapon is the cobblestone, as we suspected, but the angle of the blow is odd in relationship to the placement of the body."

"Meaning . . . ?"

"Meaning, he was standing when he was struck, then our killer placed his body onto the bed of newspapers. The stone crushed the right side of his skull behind the ear. The angle doesn't work if Carson was prone."

"Okay."

"Next: Polycrates was right about the pooch. There

were no traces of dog food in Freddie's digestive tract, and we lifted canine samples from both the open can and plastic fork; also from the newspapers. We lifted no identifiable fingerprints from the scene other than Carson's."

Lever dumped sugar into his coffee, stirred, then took a long and happy swallow. "And you checked out those tire tracks?"

"Right," Jones answered. "And that's where things start getting interesting. The tread is a standard Goodyear radial, but a problem arises when we try to narrow down the vehicle's make. Ford, Chrysler, GM: all those manufacturers drop their SUVs onto oversized pickup truck frames; and that's exactly what we trace these tire tracks back to: an oversized pickup."

"But what you're saying is: The vehicle could also have been one of those tanks everyone's driving?"

"Yes. My gut tells me it was an SUV, but I won't swear to it; not yet. See, if the vehicle was a pickup truck, and the bed was empty, there would have been noticeable fishtail action when the driver punched the gas. . . . No weight over the rear wheels."

"Yeah," Lever said as Lorraine placed the BLT in front of him, "but if the truck bed wasn't empty . . . if it had some weight . . ."

"Exactly. That's why I won't swear to my SUV theory. But on the other hand, think about this: If you swing by *Dancin' Darby's Barbecue* late at night and look at the pickups lining the lot, you'll notice that nobody leaves anything in a truck bed after dark. There's no security."

"Of course, we have no reason to believe the tire tracks had anything to do with Freddie's death."

Jones smiled briefly. "Not so fast. Hold that thought while we move on to our second body: our Jane Doe. We still have no positive ID on her. Missing persons has expanded their search to include a wider radius; nothing, so far. I'm betting there's no way this woman was from the region. Point two: Carlyle says she'd been dead over forty-eight hours when we found her. We're looking at two days or more *before* the newspaper she was found lying on was even printed. It doesn't take a genius to figure out that she was dumped behind the station and did not arrive in Newcastle via bus . . . at least not on Saturday. Murder weapon? I'm working on it. It had to be something smooth—like chrome—because I've found no residue. I keep thinking golf club, but then I look at her attire, and it doesn't match. No way she just walked off the fifth green at Pinehurst."

"You gonna eat your pickle?"

"Yes, I am."

Lever groaned slightly. "What else?"

"You can ask Lorraine for another pickle, Al."

Lever shook his head. "I'm watching my waistline—"

"By giving up a second pickle?"

"You gotta start somewhere." Al sighed. "So, what else ya got?"

"Do you remember how muddy her boots were?"

"Yeah."

"At first, I figured the dirt came from the construction site near the park on Third Street, but it didn't check. In fact, the soil's not from around here."

"Where would you peg it?"

"No idea at this point, but I'm thinking west of here. Berkshires, maybe. It's organically very rich with a high clay content, i.e., it ain't city slime."

"Someone could've hauled it in . . . for a garden or backyard."

Jones shrugged. "Possibly. But, since I live on the eleventh floor, I don't immediately think gardens. Anyway, here's the kicker, here's what brings the whole thing together: I found samples of the same type of substance in the tire tracks left near Freddie Carson's body in Adams Alley."

Lever stopped chewing the last morsel of his BLT and swiveled on his stool to face Jones. "You're sure? I mean, how long does dirt stay in tires?"

"Depends on tread depth, but there was a hit-and-run case out in Ohio a year ago; pedestrian got creamed crossing the street. The driver fled the scene, then got the car fixed on the sly and sold it to some unsuspecting schmo in New York State. But the cops tracked it down on an anonymous tip nine months later. The lab boys were still able to pull the victim's DNA, hair, and blood samples from the tires."

"Jeez, remind me not to buy something with big tires. . . . So, you think Freddie was dumped there, too?"

"No. That cobblestone came from Adams Alley, and that's where Freddie was killed."

"And our Jane Doe couldn't have killed him because she died first. Any theories, Abe?"

"Not really . . . but clearly, this soil business is the best lead we have. If we can locate the SUV, identify the material caught in the tire treads, we've got something. And if that same vehicle dumped our Jane Doe behind the bus station, which I'm sure it did, we'll find traces of the same soil on the interior as well."

Lever stopped the waitress as she passed. "Lorraine, can we get a check here?"

"No pie today, Al?"

Lever shook his head, although the movement was less than assertive. "Lunch is on me, Abe. . . . Give me a lift back to the station house, will ya?"

"I can wait for you to finish your dessert, Al."

"And have Mr. Slim and Trim here counting each and every calorie? No way."

"All you need is a little aerobic—"

"Don't start, Abe. Weight rooms, power walks, jogging, *rowing,* for Pete's sake: You can have it. Exercise and I are gonna keep a healthy distance." Lever paid the tab, and the two men walked to Jones's car. After they were seated, Lever said, "Let me ask you something, Abe? The Peterman brothers: They're the managing agents for your apartment building, aren't they?"

Jones spoke as he eased his car into the traffic flow. "Well, it's a condo, and I make my maintenance checks out to a firm called Argus Enterprises. But yeah, once you sift through all the corporate mumbo-jumbo, it's the Petermans'. They built the complex to be 'integral to Newcastle's upscale waterfront renovation' . . . that's according to the initial real estate listing. Why do you ask?"

"These guys stand to gain a lot if that empowerment zone goes through. They own a number of buildings in the zone. And the first thing they'll want to get rid of are the homeless missions."

"I'm with you so far," Jones answered as he made a right turn. "I'm going to drive across on Eleventh. There's construction on Ninth Street. . . . Anyway, back to the Petermans: I don't know, Al, we're talking double homicide. The Petermans are businessmen. High-pressure? Sure. Cutthroat with competitors? I have no doubt. But killing people?"

"A lot of folks don't consider the homeless *people.*"

Abe thought. "Well . . . I'd start by finding out what kind of cars the Peterman brothers drive."

"I intend to do just that."

Jones made a right-hand turn in front of the *Crier* building and Lever said, "Whoa, whoa, hold up. Park here for a minute, will ya? There's Rosco's Jeep." He pointed. "I need to ask him something, and the bum hasn't answered his phone all day. He must be up at Belle's office."

Abe located a parking space halfway down the block from Rosco's car. He flipped his sun visor down to display a Newcastle Police Department identification card, and the two men walked back to the Jeep. Lever reached across the hood, pulled a parking ticket from under the wiper blade, and laughed.

"I can't wait to hand him this. It's a good one, too: twenty-five smacks." He slid the ticket into his jacket. "I'll only be about five minutes. Do you want to come in or wait out here?"

"I'll wait."

Lever was actually gone for almost fifteen minutes. When he returned, he wasn't smiling. "I don't know where this bozo's gotten to. I phoned his apartment, his office . . ." Al cocked his thumb toward the *Crier* building. "Belle's not at the newspaper offices, and no one knows where she is. The answering machine picked up at her home. I'll tell ya, Abe, this is what drove me crazy when me and Polly—crates were partners. You never knew what the hell he was up to."

"Looks like whatever terrain he was tackling, he was up to his ears in mud."

"Huh?"

"Take a peek at his tires."

Lever glanced at the Jeep's tires. All four were caked in reddish brown soil. "Where'd he pick that up, do you think?"

"I don't know," Abe said as he pulled a plastic bag from his pocket, "but I don't like what I see." He bent down, took samples of the dirt, and placed them into the bag. "I think you should have this vehicle impounded, Al. If Rosco's around, it's the fastest way to get his attention. . . . But I have a real bad feeling that Rosco's not around."

"What makes you say that?"

"When have you ever known him to get a parking ticket?" Abe reached into the Jeep and flipped down the sun visor. Attached to it was the same Newcastle Police Department identification card Jones kept in his own car.

"How'd he get one of those?"

"Friends on the force?"

Lever only shook his head.

Jones didn't speak for a long minute. "I gotta tell you, Al, this mud is bothering me."

Lever didn't respond; instead, he continued to stare at the Jeep.

"It looks like the same type of soil we found on the dead woman and in Adams Alley."

"You sure about that?"

"I'll run tests, Al. But at this point, I'd stake my rep on it."

Lever walked to Abe's car and radioed the station house. "Al Lever," he said the moment the line was answered. "I've got an abandoned vehicle I want impounded. I want it done now."

CHAPTER

21

Al Lever wiped his feet on the doormat lying on Belle's sunny front porch. Not once or twice, but three times. As he scraped his shoes, his hand reached first for the brass knocker, then the doorbell, and finally withdrew. After a minute, he stood still and composed himself. He knew he had to inform Belle; there was no escaping that fact. Better to be businesslike about the situation. Better to take the bull by the horns.

He raised his hand again, opting for the bell as being less harsh. He heard the sound echo through the house, then Belle's voice calling a relieved: "Rosco? Where have you been!? I'll be there in a sec!"

Lever's facial muscles tightened. Being a cop could be hard as hell at times like this.

Belle opened the door. "Al!" Her smiling face registered swift disappointment that it was not her fiancé on the porch, then transformed itself into a facsimile of polite welcome, and finally metamorphosed into outright dread. "Is Rosco . . . ?" was all she said.

"Do you mind if I come in?"

Belle stood aside and held the door.

"We found his Jeep. . . ."

Belle studied Lever's expression. Visions of Western Union telegrams—the kind that informed a distraught wife she'd lost her husband in some far-off, war-torn land—flew through her head. She didn't speak for a long minute. When she did, her voice was hushed. "Are you telling me that Rosco's been hurt?"

Al put his hand on her shoulder. "No. . . . No. I'm telling you we found his car; that's all. No sign of blood, no sign of struggle. The vehicle has mud embedded in the tires . . . a lot of it."

Belle wrapped her arms around herself but otherwise remained still and silent. Al had been through this gruesome routine many times before. Family, friends: everyone leapt to the worst-case scenario. Either that, or they went into full denial mode. Belle was obviously of the face-up-to-a-terrible-reality school.

"Meaning?" she finally asked.

"Meaning that he was on the trail of something that took him out of the city—"

Belle shook her head as she interrupted. "He didn't check in last night."

"Does he usually?"

"Yes. . . . Actually, I'd assumed we'd have supper together, celebrate getting our marriage license . . ."

Lever accepted the information but didn't offer an explanation. "Why don't we sit down for a minute."

She led the way into her office. "Can I get you something? Some tea or coffee?"

"Thanks, no." Almost unconsciously, he patted his breast pocket and cigarette pack, then was glad Belle hadn't noticed the gesture.

"This is an official visit, isn't it, Al? Meeting with the fiancée to share distressing news . . ." Belle perched nervously on the edge of her desk while Al sank heavily into one of the black and white deck chairs.

"We don't have any corroborative evidence, Belle, just a car with mud-caked tires. I was hoping you could supply some missing pieces to the story."

She thought. "That's the second time you've mentioned mud, Al. Is there something you're not telling me?"

Lever hesitated, then plunged ahead. "Abe Jones feels the soil samples might connect the Carson death to the woman behind the bus depot. It's his feeling that the traces he lifted from the dead woman's shoes and the tire tracks left at the Carson site are from the same locale. 'Organically rich with a high clay content' is the term he used; in other words, country dirt."

Belle walked across her office. Outside, the sun was shining and the air warming in anticipation of summer. The world was green and gold, the sky a limitless blue. How could there be problems on such a fine May day? How could she contemplate Rosco being in danger, perhaps even—? She cut off the thought and turned back to face Al.

"I received a very disturbing crossword puzzle this morning . . . plus a couple of perplexing telephone calls. No, they were more than perplexing; they were downright unsettling. . . ."

Lever made a few notes on a small pad of paper, then interjected, "Someone phoned here. Would you categorize it as a threat?"

"That's just it. The call came to Cleo's house. I received the cryptic there, too. She'd gotten a message stating Rosco was 'missing in action.' She contacted me immediately; I drove to her home. . . ." Belle described the full circle of events, including the cell phone call from Geoffrey Wright's truck.

Lever frowned. "If the contractor hadn't beamed in, you would have been able to trace the previous message. Damn!"

"That's what I thought, too." Belle's expression remained grave.

"I don't like the fact that you were contacted at Cleo's home."

"I didn't, either. Actually, it gave me the creeps . . . as if someone had followed me. I tried to reassure Cleo, but . . ."

Lever made another note. "Can you describe the caller?"

"Well . . . my first inclination was that I was speaking to a recording. There was something almost robotic in the delivery and pitch . . . but a machine can't carry on a conversation—"

"That's not entirely correct, Belle. There are recordings designed to simulate dialogue. Nine times out of ten there's extortion involved."

Belle considered this. "When the person phoned again, we had a definite conversation. But, no, I couldn't tell you whether the speaker was male or female. The accent was equally impossible to trace. Extortion? I don't know. . . . Rosco and I are hardly zillionaires—"

"Rosco assumed that the crossword you received on Sunday in the empty rose box was a stalker/obsessive fan situation, didn't he?"

Belle nodded. "But the one placed in my car this morning was definitely targeting Rosco."

Again, Al instinctively reached for his cigarettes, then pulled his hand away from his shirt pocket.

"You can smoke if you want, Al."

"No way, José. I don't want to catch any grief from Polly—crates when he comes waltzing home."

Both were silent. Finally, Belle resumed the discussion. "You asked Rosco to look into the vandalism at the homeless shelter. . . ."

Lever nodded.

"And you did so because our local real estate mavens have friends in very high places, City Council, as I recall. What I'm getting at is this: Do you think the Peterman brothers are behind the deaths of Carson and the woman at the bus depot? And if they are, is Rosco's disappearance part of the same situation?"

"Abe's condo complex is owned by the Petermans," Al answered. "He insists they run a legitimate business . . . tough, but legitimate."

"That's what they said about J. J. Hill, Al. And J. P. Morgan, and Frick. Upstanding citizens, all of them. But there were a lot of people who suffered when they got in the way of those gentlemen's business practices."

"That doesn't mean murder, Belle. A lot of people believe the Petermans' interests have been very good for Newcastle."

"If you settle a strike by equipping Pinkerton guards with rifles, what do you call the death of an unarmed man? All I'm saying is that the world hasn't changed with the advent of a new century. If anything, we're even less ethical than we were before."

Lever stood and walked to her side. "I think you should

stay with someone else for a couple of days, Belle. I'm not crazy about the idea of you here by yourself."

"Rosco said the same thing." Belle's tone had become dangerously wistful.

Al attempted a note of levity. "And you immediately agreed, right?"

"That's me. Little Miss Do-As-You're-Told."

"Seriously . . . Would you consider staying with Cleo? Or maybe Mrs. B.?"

Belle's gray eyes grew wide. "You mean bunk in with Queen Sara?" She laughed briefly, but the sound had a hollow ring. "I'll consider it." Then she turned serious again. "Rosco and I are getting married Saturday, Al. . . ."

Lever searched for words of comfort. "Your wedding will come off without a hitch, Belle. You have my word on it." But he knew she was too smart to fool. Rosco was missing, and the evidence wasn't pointing to an easy or pleasant solution.

CHAPTER

22

"Madam is in the garden."

As she ushered Belle into the foyer of White Caps, Sara Crane Briephs' ancestral home, Emma's smile was ebullient.

"Mrs. Briephs will be delighted to see you, Miss Belle. Your visits always do her a world of good."

It was useless asking Emma to drop the title *miss;* requesting less formal treatment would be tantamount to suggesting Sara's long-time maid don a sweat suit in place of her black taffeta uniform with its starched white apron and lacy collar. She and her mistress were too old school, and probably too hidebound, to change.

"Thanks, Emma. Don't trouble yourself. I can find the way myself."

"Oh, it's no trouble at all, miss."

Emma led Belle through a house remarkable in its loving devotion to the past. Damask draperies, Persian carpets, silver and crystal vases, richly waxed wood floors, polished mahogany occasional tables, and the hush that pervades a building with sturdy walls and a sturdier pedigree: Belle might have been treading through a Victorian-era home updated to the 1920s. The fact that Sara Briephs deemed the place cozy revealed a great deal about how she and her brother had been raised.

"Madam has been fretting about the weather for your wedding festivities, Miss Belle, but I believe the last day and a half have taken a considerable turn for the better. May can be an uncertain month."

Belle bit her lip. She began to appreciate how difficult it had been for Al to break the news about finding Rosco's abandoned Jeep. "Yes, it can," she said at last.

"I hope you and Mr. Rosco will be very happy," Emma added. "I know you will be."

Belle pasted on what she hoped was a joyous smile. "Thank you, Emma."

The maid opened the door leading to the veranda, stepped aside to withdraw, and Belle spotted Sara's erect form stationed in front of an ancient rose bush as if she were in the process of issuing a stern denunciation to an invading force of aphids, which she probably was. As disquieting as the conversation with Emma had been, Belle realized it had been nothing compared to discussing Rosco's disappearance with White Caps' redoubtable owner.

"Belle, dear! I didn't hear your car in the drive!" Sara marched toward her, a "stick" in hand (she refused to call it a cane) to aid in negotiating the lumpy, springtime ground. Half of the time, the "stick" was wielded as if an extension of its owner's indomitable arm.

Belle tried for another smile, then realized she could no longer fake it. "Rosco's missing," she blurted out instead.

"What do you mean, 'missing'? It's not like the boy to get cold feet, Belle. You know he's as anxious to marry you as you are to wed him."

"I mean that Al Lever and Abe Jones found Rosco's Jeep, mud-spattered and ticketed . . . but no Rosco. In fact, from the illegal parking fine, the car had been sitting there for some time."

Sara looked aghast. "What is Albert's assessment of the situation?" She wavered once, her body swaying slightly, then forced herself to stand even straighter. At length she said, "I'll sit, if you don't mind." She turned toward a carved stone bench. "Be a good girl, and come and sit down beside me."

Belle did as requested, then began describing Abe Jones's suspicion that the soil samples taken from the two crime sites might well match the mud in Rosco's tires. She also included the attack on the homeless shelter, Rosco's outrage at the vandalism, and his decision to help find the miscreants.

Sara's face grew more and more pensive. "Unsavory characters," she said after a moment. "The Petermans *and* all the johnny-come-latelies who are trying to buy up this town."

"Abe Jones stated his belief that the Petermans' business dealings are on the up and up."

"Similar remarks were made about J. J. Hill and Mr. Morgan!"

Belle smiled, and Sara regarded her with a proud and critical eye. "I realize your generation may view my references as antediluvian, young lady, but history should teach us *not* to repeat past mistakes."

"I'm smiling because I used the exact same example when I spoke with Al."

The older lady's fine silvery eyebrows arched in bemused pleasure. "Good girl! We'll turn you into an autocratic *grande dame* yet. . . . Of course, you have several decades in which to practice."

Belle took Sara's hand, and for several moments the two sat silently side by side: Belle, blond-haired, lithe; Sara, once taller, now whittled by age, white-coiffed and still determinedly slim. Belle represented Sara in youth; Sara was an image of Belle grown old.

"I'm not happy about this situation," White Caps' owner finally said.

"I'm not either," was Belle's quiet answer.

"What can I do to help, dear?"

Belle hesitated before responding. "Sara, you have entrée to the high and mighty of this city—"

"I should say so! The Crane family helped build Newcastle several hundred years ago."

"And so you'd be able to *surreptitiously* delve into the Peterman brothers' connections: political, business, et cetera—"

"Are we discussing influence peddling or something more serious, Belle dear?"

"I don't know, Sara—"

"I should apprise my brother, the senator. . . . His hometown, his state . . . Imagine the negative press if it were discovered that—"

"Not yet, Sara. Although you can certainly make use of Senator Crane's privileged information, if it's available."

"I'll make sure that it is." Sara paused, her quick brain missing nothing. "However, I sense you're not being entirely candid with me. I detect a truant element in your tale. The Petermans may be shady characters, they may even have criminal ties, but are you suggesting . . . I amend my query. Are you *intimating* that they could be responsible for Rosco's disappearance?"

Belle's face wrinkled into a frown. "I don't know, Sara. . . . But I *do* know that Rosco's gone, without a word; that two people died, most probably victims of foul play; and that the Petermans have a great deal to gain if the homeless missions are forced to relocate. And that Rosco took off after two goons he believed were hired by the Petermans."

Sara was silent a long time, although the garden fauna continued to burble in unconcerned ecstasy. "I don't like this situation, Belle," she finally said. "I don't like it one little bit."

"A seven-letter word for illness?" The voice demanding the answer was rough and angry; cruelty lurked beneath its surface.

"Disease," Belle replied, trying to gauge whether her mysterious phone mate were a man or a woman.

"Disease. Specific."

"Malaria, typhoid, rubeola, leprosy, anthrax, cholera—"

"Eight letters! And be quick about it."

"Beriberi, smallpox." She paused, counting in her head. "Jaundice, pellagra—"

"Good girl! You done yourself proud."

The voice belongs to a man, Belle decided. An educated male with an affinity for street jargon. She looked through her home office windows; the day was now waning, and although, as Emma had observed, the weather had turned mild, a spring night in Massachusetts was apt to be chilly. And Rosco was out in it. Somewhere. Somewhere where mud was found. Belle's brain started whirring. "Mud season." That was what native Vermonters called springtime. "Where's Rosco?" she suddenly demanded.

In answer, the man sneered derisively. "Wouldn't you like to know? Let's try some more linguistic calisthenics first. And then *maybe* I'll supply a little much-needed information . . . *maybe*. Criminal, *Bellisima*. Eight letters."

"Gangster," she recited evenly. "Scofflaw, garroter, fugitive, murder—"

"Evil . . . Annabella!"

"First tell me where Rosco is." Her voice held firm, but the hand clutching the receiver trembled with tension and fear.

" 'Christ walks on the black water. In black Mud

" 'Darts the Kingfisher. On Corpus Christi heart,

" 'Over the drum-beat of St. Stephen's choir . . . '

"Visceral images, no? Now, I know you're a poetry buff, *Belle bambina*. Can you name the author?" The man made a ticking sound like a clock counting seconds on a TV game show.

"Robert Traill Spence Lowell," Belle murmured half under her breath.

"I didn't hear you, sweet pea!"

"Robert Traill Spence Lowell . . . born in 1917—"

"Good girl. I'm impressed. Now, let's do evil, *ma petite belle*, as an adjective. Eight letters. And remember, speed is essential."

"Diabolic . . ." Belle began. She ran a hand across her brow; her head hurt. "Infernal, fiendish, heinous—"

"Heinous is seven letters! No dice! I thought you were a smart cookie. Too bad. I'll be saying bye-bye, now." A singsong sound like an alarm on a cheap wristwatch crackled through the wire.

"Please," Belle interrupted. "You know where Rosco is.

Please. . . . Whatever's going on with the homeless mission . . . and . . . Freddie Carson . . . and the woman behind the bus depot . . . Rosco doesn't have any additional information—"

The man laughed viciously again. "That's what you think, honey bun!"

Tears of anger sprang up in Belle's eyes. "Where is he?"

"Heinous, there's an interesting word. Let's try its derivation before we proceed. Ready, Belle?"

Her mouth went dry. She stumbled over the words. "French. *Haïr,* to hate. *Haine,* hatred."

"Nice." The man's voice warbled another botched song, ending with an off-key rendition of "The Wedding March." "What do you say we switch topics, *Bella?* The subject is Daniel Webster for one hundred all-important points."

"Please," Belle begged. "We need to discuss—"

"Daniel Webster," was the furious reply.

"A statesman," she began. "An extraordinary orator, a member of the United States Senate—"

"Secretary of State under William Henry Harrison . . . Old 'Tippecanoe and Tyler, too!' The famous 'log cabin and hard-cider' campaign . . . Do you have this information at your fingertips, Annabella? No, of course you don't. You may be facile with words; you may profess a love of poetry, but your knowledge is far from encyclopedic!" A laugh followed this outburst, after which the man hummed another garbled tune and finally commenced speaking again. "Dogs . . . Now, there's another interesting subject. The harrier: that's a breed of English hound that's been around since Norman days . . . the Bouvier des Flandres; the Kuvasz, originally Hungarian . . . likewise, the puli: good at herding . . . the Mexican hairless. . . . Have you ever seen a Tibetan mastiff?"

Belle didn't respond, and her caller again shifted gear, becoming even more bullying and demanding.

"Now, you know what I want you to do, little bell? I want you to make *me* a crossword . . . nice and symmetrical so's I can fold it in quarters, eighths, even, and have each itty, bitty piece match. You got that?"

"You have to tell me where Rosco is first—"

"Wrong answer! Tit for tat, *Bellisima*. When you're finished, you stick it under your doormat . . . No . . . better yet, put it on the porch floor with a leg of your wicker bench holding it in place. Got it?"

"Yes. But how will Rosco—?"

"It's six o'clock or thereabouts. I'll give you till eleven—"

Belle gasped.

"Not as good as you think you are, eh cutie pie? Okay, midnight's your deadline. Like the song says . . . Gonna let it all *bang* out. . . . Oh, and a theme . . . What was my last puzzle? 'Not Dreaming,' right? Ole Papa Poe, E.A.P. . . . 'Helen, thy beauty is to me' . . . and all that other gobbledygook."

Belle nodded soundlessly, then managed to whisper, "You want me to create a crossword?"

"Let's call it 'Stand By Your Man.' You should have a whole heap of inspiration for that clever game! Oh, and let's keep our little tricks to ourselves. For your sweetie's sake . . . 'All's well that ends well,' as the sages say. Don't be late. Remember, your *dead* line is midnight." The man sang what sounded like a dirge and was suddenly gone.

Belle replaced the receiver and sat staring at the phone one moment too long, because as she reached for the dial pad to trace the number, the phone rang. She jumped convulsively, then gritted her teeth. "Yes?"

"Belle, it's Al. What happened? You sound terrible." ·

The words came out before she could stop them. "Some crazy person has kidnapped Rosco! I was just about to try and trace the call."

Lever remained silent for the merest second. "I'll be right over."

"No, the house is being watched!"

"I can't let you—"

"You have to, Al. . . . Look, I've got to go. I have to construct a crossword for this nut case! He's given me six hours."

"Is there a drop—?"

"Al! I shouldn't even be talking to you." She groaned in fearful frustration. "Okay . . . I have to—" Belle stopped herself. "No, I can't tell you—"

"I'll order surveillance—"

"You can't, Al! The guy'll see you! He's probably watching right now. . . . I've got to go."

Across

1. ET craft
4. Gov. shipping regulator
7. MD airport
10. ———to tango
13. Actor Mineo
14. Cheer
15. Turn bad
16. Owns
17. Philadelphia suburb
19. Faulkner haunt
21. "Three Dog Night" hit
23. Smell
25. Unscripted line
26. French city
29. French impressionist
31. Wind dir.
32. Type of cord
33. Florida city
35. Stuns with noise
37. Vietnamese city
38. Mark of a criminal?
39. Uncovers
43. New Hampshire capital
47. Climbing vine
48. "———for Two"
50. Prometheus's brother
51. 18-Down, e.g.
52. Florida city
54. Logical beginning?
55. John B. Bogart news flash?
58. Everyone has one
60. New York campus
63. Towel word
64. Wind dir.
65. Three-match link
66. War stat.
67. Ran into
68. Ref. work

69. Water on the grass
70. Stitch

Down

1. Loc. of 43-Across and 43-Down
2. "Bad news travels fast and———
   —," Plutarch
3. Crank
4. "———Here to Eternity"
5. Klaus———Brandauer
6. New York neighborhood
7. Sulked
8. "Look Homeward, Angel" author
9. News tidbit
10. Skater's woe
11. Existed
12. CIA predecessor
18. Picture of Olivier?
20. Seagal or Stallone, e.g.
22. ———& yang
23. Unusual
24. Some feds
27. Fire
28. Some Chicago trains
30. March King
32. Ms. White
34. Born
36. Tokyo once
39. Sprite
40. Caesar's dozen
41. Seer
42. Soiled
43. Provincetown locale
44. Heirloom jewelry
45. Actress Charlotte
46. Brit. decoration
49. Hosp. employee
52. Butcher's cut
53. Together

STAND BY YOUR MAN

56. El———
57. Sketch
58. Resistance unit
59. Easy as———
61. Fib
62. "L.A.———"

CHAPTER

23

"But why did you do it, Al? The guy specifically told me not to share information with anyone. You set up a surveillance team. I just don't see the rationale behind the decision."

It was six-forty-five A.M., the sky beginning to glow blue and pink, but the two faces that stared across Belle's desk looked far from glowing and healthy. Belle hadn't slept a wink, but then neither had Al.

"If you'd *informed* me the drop site was going to be your front porch, I would have played the scenario a lot differently, Belle—"

"The guy told me not to—"

"Let's get a couple of facts straight. One: I'm on your side, and I want to find Rosco just as much as you do. Two: I'm not going to let my best buddy's fiancée wrestle with some psycho I have every reason to believe is stalking her—"

"It's not me he's after."

"You don't know that, Belle! And besides, remember Rosco's supposition was that *you* were the target, not him."

"But a surveillance team, Al—"

"Undercover, Belle . . . Sewer repair trucks are out at all hours. This is an old city. The mains and secondary pipes break all the time—"

"I know this weirdo spotted something wrong, Al. I'm not blaming you for trying to help, but I'm convinced that's why he didn't show." Belle ran her hand wearily over the unretrieved cryptic. Fatigue made her eyes water. She didn't remember when she'd last eaten or even had a drink of water.

"You *are* blaming me, Belle. And you're angry and upset . . . and worried. So am I. But this is police protocol. I made a decision based on facts. Incomplete, as it turns out . . . But what have we got here? Homicide—a probable double—and a potential kidnapping. . . . Now, what am I supposed to do? Sit around and wait for this goon to strike again? Whoever nabbed Rosco would have no trouble tackling you—"

"Because I'm female?" Belle's voice and jaw were tight.

"Because you probably weigh only a hundred and ten pounds. That's not a lot of beef to throw against a male who's attacking you."

Belle was quiet for a long minute. "So, what do we do now?"

"Wait until you're recontacted."

"He won't call if he knows you're here."

"I guarantee that's not the case." Al's voice was calm, professional, kind. Belle found herself desperately wanting to believe him. "These sickos thrive on police attention. Trust me."

Belle closed her eyes, then slowly opened them. "Do you want some coffee, Al?"

"Love some."

As they headed for the kitchen, Lever picked up the crossword. "How do you do these things?" His manner had a false heartiness that tried to say, *Don't worry. It's going to be okay.*

Belle tried to match the tone. "State secret." She added an equally disingenuous, "I hope you like your coffee strong."

"You know what they say? If a spoon stands up in it . . ." Al examined the cryptic. " 'Stand By Your Man' . . . Oh, I get it, you put the word *man* throughout the puzzle."

"18-Down," Belle recited. "MARATHON MAN; 55-Across: MAN BITES DOG; 21-Across: FAMILY OF MAN . . . I can recite this thing in my sleep—"

"Which you didn't get."

"Which I didn't get. Are you certain this guy will make another attempt with you here, Al?"

"I'd stake my badge on it. There was nothing you recognized in the man's inflection? A regional dialect? Odd speech pattern?"

"Nothing other than what I already shared with you: a tin ear, and a disconcerting habit of switching from erudite to undereducated language and locution—"

"Which could mean a schizophrenic . . ."

Belle poured coffee into two mugs and looked at the clock on the stove. "It's after seven."

"He'll call, Belle. Guys like this can't stay away."

As if on cue, the phone rang. Al banged his mug on the countertop, spilling a quarter of the black brown liquid on the surface. He held up a hand and motioned for Belle to wait until he reached the office extension.

Three endless rings elapsed before he shouted the all clear, and they picked up the receivers in unison. "Hello?" Belle realized her voice sounded hideously unnatural. If the mystery man didn't already know she had company, he'd certainly guess from her tone.

"Annabella Graham?" The male voice was nervous. Belle had a difficult time pegging it as the self-confident caller of thirteen hours earlier. Schizophrenia, she reminded herself.

"The puzzle's done," she said, "but I . . . I . . . Just tell me what to do with it now."

A tense pause greeted her. "This is Annabella Graham, isn't it?"

Belle swallowed. "This is she." She considered asking about Rosco but decided to follow the caller's lead. "This is Annabella Graham."

"I apologize for phoning so early. . . ."

Belle stretched the cord as far as she could but was unable to see past the door to the living room and beyond. "That's all right."

"But working folk have such nasty schedules—"

"Look, mister—"

"Oh! Russ Parrotti, here. I'm sorry; I should have introduced myself right off the bat. Russ Parrotti of the *Boston Sentinel*. Parrotti, not Perot, and Russ rather than Ross." The man named Russ laughed. Belle did not. "Miss Graham, I'm fact-checking a story on you by one of our contributors, an Elise Elliott—"

"What?"

"I'm a fact-checker with the *Sentinel*. And, again, Miss Graham, I apologize for the inconvenience of the hour, but—"

"Look, Mr. Parrot—"

"Parrotti—"

"Mr. Parrotti. You have to get off this line. I'm expecting a crucial call." Belle slammed the receiver down without waiting for a response. Lever joined her a moment later.

"Not him?"

She shook her head, then reflexively began mopping up spilled coffee.

"You're sure?"

Belle turned horrified eyes on Al.

"I'm going to trace the call, just in case." He pounded numbers on the dial pad, wrote down the results, called Boston information, and copied the *Sentinel*'s main number. "Looks like Russ Parrotti may be on the up and up."

"What do you mean, 'may be'?"

"Crazies often like to exist inconspicuously, working the quietest jobs. It's like camouflage."

"But Parrotti's in Boston—"

"Which is an hour away, max."

Belle's shoulders sagged. She felt on the verge of tears. She was about to answer when the phone rang a second time. Al bolted toward the office extension, but before he was halfway through the living room, Belle grabbed the receiver.

"My number's unlisted. Now, lose the cop." Then came a loud and final click.

"That's all right. No trouble," Belle said as Al picked up, adding a falsely serene, "Wrong number" for his benefit.

Then she replaced the receiver in the cradle, affixed a determined smile, and greeted the returning Lever with a pleasant: "You know what, Al? We're both starving, and the cupboards are bare. How about if I sit here by the phone while you visit the mom-and-pop store on the corner and get us some eggs?" She stopped herself as if a truth had suddenly dawned. "Darn it! They won't be open this early. You'll have to drive over to the supermarket—"

"I'm not leaving, Belle. And I'm not hungry."

"But I am, Al. Look, I won't answer the phone till you get back. How's that?"

Al thought. "Takeout from Lawson's would be easier and faster. Maybe some French toast . . . a mushroom omelette . . ."

Belle's smile grew as she counted minutes in her head. Round trip to the café would take twenty to thirty minutes *if* the morning's orders were light. "Sounds good to me."

"What'll you have?"

"You choose, Al. I've given up making decisions."

When the phone rang again, Belle was ready.

"I'll try," she said in answer to the caller's abrupt request. "It's a newspaper, and I'm only the—"

A stream of oaths interrupted her, which was followed by another question.

"I'll do my best. I promise. . . . But what about Rosco?"

"I'm still thinking, little Annabel Lee . . .

" 'In her sepulchre there by the sea—

" 'In her tomb by the sounding sea.' Poe, again . . . You hurry on down to the *Crier*, and then we'll powwow again, Annabel."

CHAPTER

24

At first meeting, Kit hadn't been sure about Rosco. To begin with, he was the only human being the dog had encountered who'd refused to respond, pro or con, to a friendly face-licking. He'd remained motionless when the puppy had run her wet tongue over his stubbled cheeks; never blinking his eyes or rolling his head to one side, let alone knocking her halfway across the room and shouting, "Get lost, will ya?"

The reason for this comatose state, a reason Kit was unaware of, was that Rosco had been fed a dose of methylmorphine thirty-six hours earlier. But he wasn't dead; in fact, despite the chill of the basement room, his body had retained its warmth, allowing the puppy to curl up beside him through two cold nights, which was lucky for both of them, as the building had been without heat for some time.

However, by eleven A.M., the sun was again high enough in the sky to begin filtering in through the only link to the outside world: a small, rectangular window at the juncture of the ceiling and wall. Looking up and out through the dirty glass would have required standing on a chair, but its position in the wall didn't impede the welcome light. In fact, it created a pleasant warm spot on the old dirt floor, and since Rosco was proving to be a decidedly dull companion, Kit had opted to take advantage of the radiant heat, curling up in a tight ball beneath the sun's mellow rays. She'd just started to nod off when Rosco finally showed signs of life by letting out an extended and painful groan. Kit leapt to her feet, trotted over to him, and once again began licking his face.

"Arrrgh . . ." Rosco shook his head and made an aborted attempt to wipe the wetness from his face. The fact that his hands had been bound behind his back with duct tape, and that his ankles were also strapped together made the effort less than successful. Through the dense fog that was his gradually recovering brain, he imagined himself turned into a gigantic and bloated earthworm, one that felt bruised and sore all over. He pictured an enormous fishhook, himself as bait, and the cold plunge in the frigid ocean.

Rosco groaned again, slept again, then slowly reawakened. He rolled to one side, forcing himself to inch his way up the wall until he settled into a crabbed and uncomfortable sitting position. "Okay," he muttered with his eyes shut tight. "I'm alive. Nice start."

Kit took the words as a sign of good humor, jumping into his lap, placing her paws on his chest, and licking determinedly his face. Rosco opened his eyes briefly, stared at the dog, then closed them again, trying to remember how he'd come to be tied up in an icy and evil-smelling basement with only a dog for company. The two guys who tried to trash the homeless mission, he finally remembered through the haze, Belle's mystery crossword, the empty rose box . . . and Freddie Carson. The picture gradually came into focus.

Rosco opened his eyes. "How are ya, Kit?" He blinked several times and shook his head in an effort to calibrate his thoughts. His head pounded fiercely. "I don't suppose you have any coffee around here? Or a couple of aspirin?"

Again, she licked his face.

"A cell phone would be too much to ask, right?"

Kit responded with a low whimper, while Rosco's chin dropped suddenly toward his chest. A wave of nausea attacked him, then receded little by little.

"How about a knife? Straight razor? Or maybe you could chew this tape from my wrists?"

Kit skipped from his lap, crossed back to the sunny spot, and barked, suggesting it might be a better place to spend the day.

Rosco groaned for a third time; his mouth, he realized, felt as if a dentist had padded it with wads of cotton and left them there. "You wouldn't have any idea how to get out of here, would you, Kit?"

He looked around in an attempt to get his bearings, but nothing about the place seemed remotely familiar. Old stone walls, an open-timbered ceiling, a hard-packed dirt floor that had probably been there for a hundred years. He could have been on Ninth Street or in Alaska for all he knew. Rosco twisted his hands to the left side of his torso and peered at his wristwatch. It took a beat for the date and time to register in his conscious thoughts. "It's Wednesday . . . ? What happened to Tuesday?"

Kip barked again.

"Have you been here since Tuesday, too?" Rosco studied the room, noting for the first time the many bowls of half-eaten kibble, the water left in mismatched pots, the newspapers serving as dog toilets. "I guess we've both been consigned to the dungeon. . . ."

He placed his feet flat on the floor and began working his back up the wall until he was standing: wobbly and in pain but erect. His head felt worse than it had when he'd been sitting. His first instinct was that someone had clobbered him. He moved his jaw from side to side; the ache in his temples increased, and another spasm of nausea attacked him. Rosco let it pass, then hopped to the door, turned around until his hands reached the doorknob, and grasped it. It wouldn't budge. He yanked hard, but the door was locked, its movement so restricted, he assumed it was bolted from the other side.

"What do you think, Kit, if I scream my head off, the cops will be here in no time?"

The puppy cocked her head to one side, producing a look of confusion.

"Never mind, it was a rhetorical question."

Rosco moved slowly back across the room and attempted to look up through the window. He saw metal grating and sky but nothing else that would indicate whether the basement's locale was in some deserted part of Newcastle, the burbs, or deep in the country. He noted there was no exterior noise, or if there was, it was too faint to hear. By the absence of sirens, grinding bus gears, and irate horn blasts, he guessed city living was no longer a consideration.

"Well, Kit, looks like we're here for a while. I don't suppose you have a deck of cards?"

Since Kit had no tail to speak of, the act of wagging what there was only served to make her hindquarters jounce around like a kite in the wind. But she seemed very happy; Rosco wasn't such a dud after all.

CHAPTER

25

Belle stepped off the elevator on the fifth floor of the *Crier* building and, as usual, the offices were chaotic: editors racing from door to door, barking brusque questions about their reporters' abilities to fill pages intelligently or their combined reluctance to drop a well-chosen line of text, grilling fact-checkers, muttering about possible lawsuits, and hollering out deadlines. "Check the clock, people, check the clock!" was the favored dictum on this particular Wednesday. The maelstrom was the reason Belle preferred to create her cryptics at home; silence was not one of the luxuries afforded by the *Crier* workplace.

" 'Stand by Your Man.' "

Belle snapped her head sharply to her right and stared at the person who'd spoken. "What did you say?"

" 'Stand by Your Man.' The Tammy Wynette song? That's what you were humming on the elevator. A little touchy for the bride-to-be, aren't you, Belle?"

It took her a beat to recognize the speaker as Wally, one

of the pressroom runners. She forced a careless smile. "Sorry, Wally, you're right. I guess I am a little over-stressed with the party details. I didn't even know who was talking to me. . . ."

"Hey, *no problema,* I felt the same way walking into my wedding day . . . but, hey, five years and still going strong." Wally tapped his wedding ring and winked. *"Buona fortuna, Bellissima!* Gotta run." He trotted down the hallway and ducked through the glass-paneled door of the pressroom.

Belle watched him leave, her expression turning wary again. *Bellisima,* she thought, as she walked the length of the hall to a door marked *Jerry Powers.* She knocked twice and stepped in without waiting for an answer. Like Rosco, Jerry, the *Crier*'s entertainment editor, was in his late thirties; unlike Rosco, he was panicked about approaching the dire fortieth year and was already addicted to hair dyes, gels, and absurdly expensive stylists. He was also a coffee addict.

At the moment, he was standing in front of his fax machine watching the paper spit out. When he saw he had company, his hand reflexively smoothed the moussed hair along his forehead.

"Hold on a second, will ya, Belle? They've changed the release date on the new Spielberg film. Man, I hate these last-minute modifications. Stevie, Stevie, Stevie, give me a break, will ya, pal?" Jerry tore the fax from the machine and walked to his desk. "Let me make a note about this permutation before I forget it. . . . Dontcha just love Hollywood?" He scribbled something on a desk calendar and looked up. "What's up, cute stuff?"

Belle felt her jaw begin to tense. "Jerry, I need to make a switch in today's crossword puzzle." She handed him an envelope containing the "Stand by Your Man" puzzle. "This needs to be slotted instead."

"Ho-ho-ho, hardy-har-har . . . You're kidding, right?"

"No. It's very important."

"No can do, Bellie. I can't make that kind of a change at this late date. You know that. I'm up to my ears here. First, Stevie Spielberg and then you."

"Everything's the same size, Jerry. It's a simple swap. One for one. It's been formatted. . . . Lift out the old puzzle, drop in this new one."

"Nix. I don't have the time. Nix, nix, nix."

Belle coughed slightly. "This comes down from up top."

"What are you talking about, up top?"

Belle had expected trouble. Jerry was fun to talk to, and he always had an amusing story or two, but, despite his caffeinated demeanor, he was intrinsically lazy, and she'd anticipated that he'd balk at the notion of additional work. She found herself searching for a logical explanation, one that Jerry would buy. Her mysterious caller had been adamant about the crossword appearing in Wednesday's paper. "Thus, dear Bella-Bella," he'd said, "I see the puzzle, but neither you nor your friend the cop see me."

"Look, Jerry," she said, slightly raising her voice to cover the lie, "the switch is absolutely necessary. There are legal ramifications. Legal's in on this."

"Legal? What the hell are you talking about?"

"I'm trying to save you time. I got called by *Legal* at dawn this morning. They have a problem with the cryptic I constructed for today's paper." Belle began to rack her brain in an attempt to recall which puzzle had been slated for Wednesday's *Crier*, although she realized that the odds that Jerry had looked at it were remote. "Let me explain. Today's puzzle—"

"What about it?"

"Have you studied it?"

"Ahhhh . . ."

"Never mind, it's not important, but the thing is, Legal has a problem with it and wants it pulled. There's no point in going into all the details now, but if you don't believe me, call Legal yourself." Belle knew the last thing Jerry would want to do was get on the phone with the *Crier*'s lawyers. It was a good way to kill an hour.

"You're sure about this?"

"I wouldn't be standing here wasting your time if I weren't. 'We're gonna get sued up the ying-yang' was the term used. They're sweating bullets up there."

Jerry snatched the manila envelope from her hands. "Damn, I hate these changes. Why can't Legal leave well enough alone?"

"Beats me. Hey, I had to draw up a whole new crossword for them . . . quick time."

B ack in her office, Belle closed the door and locked it, something she'd never done before, although the effort did little to mute the pandemonium issuing from the central corridor. She flopped into her chair and lay her head on the desktop. She felt like crying but knew it was useless, as well as a sign of weakness. All she could do now was wait, wait until the *Crier* hit the newsstands at four-thirty, wait for this schizoid to buy the paper, recognize the puzzle he'd asked for, and finally recontact her.

She slowly sat erect and looked at the bank building across the street. At the far eastern side of the sixth floor, seven adjoining windows, each containing a single large red block letter. Viewed together, they spelled For Rent.

"That's it," Belle said aloud. She reached for the telephone directory and began flipping through the pages. "Peterman . . . Peterman . . . ah, here we go; Peterman Brothers Real Estate—Argus Enterprises." Belle punched the numbers into her phone and waited. It was answered on the first ring.

"Argus Enterprises. How may I direct your call?"

"Yes, I noticed you have residential lofts for sale by prospectus on Fifth Street, across from Margaret House for women? I wonder if I might take a look at them?"

"Can you hold? I'll connect you with a sales consultant."

"Thank you."

Belle drummed her fingers on her desk. It seemed to take forever for a consultant to answer the line.

Finally: "This is Janice Lane, how can I help you?"

Belle repeated her request.

"Of course, Miss . . . ? Or is it Mrs. . . . ?"

"Miss . . . Miss Carol Lewis," Belle answered.

"Ahhh . . . Like Lewis Carroll, only backward. Sorry, you must get that all the time."

"Less than you might think," Belle said, surprised that Janice had jumped so quickly to the *Alice's Adventures in Wonderland* connection.

"Well, Miss Lewis, the lofts on Fifth Street will be truly spectacular living spaces when completed. Each is unique, with its own special view. The upper floors are designed to take full advantage of near-panoramic vistas of the harbor. Perhaps there's a time early next week that would be convenient for us to meet?"

"I was hoping to view them today. I'm down from Boston and would like to catch the four o'clock train back."

"I see, well . . . perhaps I could meet you there in say . . . forty-five minutes? How would that be?"

"To be honest, Miss Lane—"

"Please, call me Janice."

"Okay, but I'm only a block or two from the Peterman offices. Maybe I could meet you there? We could drive over together?"

"Well, that's a possibility, but we're going through a good deal of remodeling here; especially of the outdoor spaces. It's quite a mess. I'd hate for you to get your clothes dirty." Janice laughed. "I mean this is a *real* disaster area; not a fortuitous first impression of Argus Enterprises."

"That's all right."

"Okay, but don't say I didn't warn you. I'll see you in a half hour or so? You obviously know where the building is?"

"Yes."

"The residential real estate offices are on the penthouse level. Just tell the receptionist you're here to see me."

Belle's phone rang a few seconds later. She hesitated, torn between a desire to reconnect with the mystery puzzle constructor—if this were indeed he—and equally angered and repelled by the situation. Emotion made her clench the receiver. By the time she picked up, the overzealous operator had already shunted the call to her private voice mailbox. Belle waited a couple of minutes, then entered her code and listened to a message from a harassed Al Lever.

"Dammit, Belle, where are you? You're slipperier than Rosco . . . if that's possible. No wonder you two are getting hitched. Listen, this isn't funny. There's a dangerous loony out there. If this guy's nabbed Rosco, how hard is it going to be for him to grab you, too? I want you to check in with me ASAP, and I mean that. I'm on my way to the station house. Call me the minute you get this. Okay?"

After she hung up the phone, Belle mouthed a silent, "Sorry, Al."

* * *

In reality, the *Crier* offices weren't close to the Petermans' headquarters, and Belle was hard pressed to get
there in a half hour. From the exterior, the structure looked
like any other post–World War II office building in Newcastle: nondescript brick, with rows of utilitarian windows
that lacked both style and visual definition. The lobby was
equally bland, although it was obvious that serious renova-
tions were under way. A black and white marble floor was
crisscrossed with runners of heavy brown paper, while a
layer of grit covered everything.

Belle walked to the elevator bank, stepped into a waiting car, and pressed the button marked PH, then rode alone
up seventeen floors to the penthouse. When the doors
opened, she was greeted with a smell that seemed to blend
new paint with freshly tilled farmland. A voice yelled,
"Hey, Stu, these drawings call for six rhodies, not eight."

Belle stepped off the elevator, waited for a worker to
pass with a wheelbarrow full of dirt, and approached the
reception desk. "I'm Bel—" She coughed. "Sorry, I must
have picked up some dust."

The receptionist smiled. "Don't worry, honey, this place
has been a mess for a month now. They're redoing the ter-
race. It's gonna look like the Amazon jungle by the time
they're done. You wait and see."

"I'll bet." Belle watched a man wheel a young, multi-
trunked white birch from the service elevator and head down
the hallway toward a door that opened onto the roof deck.
"I'm here to see Janice Lane. My name is . . . Carol Lewis."

"Oh, sure, she's expecting you. Just follow that tree.
Her office is the last door on the left. I'll buzz and tell her
you're on your way."

As Belle approached the last door, Janice stepped out. She was slightly taller and older than Belle, a striking-looking African-American, with long hair braided into one thick plait and tied elaborately behind her neck. She extended her hand, and Belle immediately felt guilty for lying about her name and her desire to purchase a residential property.

"I'm Janice, Miss Lewis—"

"Please call me Carol."

"Fine." Janice tilted her head in the direction of several moving trees and smiled warmly. "I told you we were inhabiting a work in progress. You can see why I wanted to meet over on Fifth Street."

"Well, I was just around the corner." Belle also smiled. "What's going on out there?" She nodded toward the windows behind Janice's desk. On the terrace, eight or nine workers were carting dirt, planting trees, shrubs, and perennials, and constructing various levels of wooden walkways, arbors, and trellises. It looked as if they were trying to re-create a country garden—and succeeding.

"Ohh . . ." Janice said with a sigh, "the Petermans got tired of the old landscaping. I hate to say it, but they just tossed out the original plantings. We employees weren't too happy . . . especially those of us with green thumbs. I saved a few plants for myself, but it's their building . . . and it's going to be spectacular when the project's finished. The old soil had been expended. That's why it's such a mess; the landscapers had to replace it with new dirt brought down from the farm in New Hampshire . . . truck-loads of the stuff."

"Whose farm?"

"The younger Mr. Peterman. Otto. He has a large place near Plymouth. It's supposed to be beautiful. Anyway, why don't we take my car for our tour? You can look at the brochure and the financials on the way. How's that? I think you'll be very impressed with what you see."

"Sounds great. You must have quite a view here. Would it be all right if I stepped outside and took a look?"

"If you don't mind getting a little dirt on you."

Janice led the way out to the roof deck. It covered the entire south end of the building, measuring fifty feet by seventy feet, and seemed to encompass all of Newcastle in its view, with Buzzards Bay stretching out to the horizon.

"This is some undertaking," Belle said.

"It is. Mr. Peterman considers himself quite the horti-culturist."

Belle reached into one of the large concrete planters, picked up a small clump of fresh earth, and brought it to her nose. "Hmmm, there's nothing like the smell of coun-try dirt. After living in a city so long, we forget."

Janice laughed. "You sound just like Otto Peterman."

"Janice!" an agitated voice called from across the ter-race. "This is a restricted area. No one but employees al-lowed until we complete construction."

A tall man in his late fifties approached quickly. He wore expensive suit pants and braces over a hand-made shirt; he had the aura of someone who had come from nothing and become very wealthy the hard way. Belle slipped the piece of earth into her pocket and struggled to one-handedly wrap it in a folded tissue.

"I'm sorry, Mr. Peterman," Janice said. "This is Miss Lewis. I'm showing her the Fifth Street property, but she asked to see your garden first."

Otto Peterman extended his hand to Belle. "Miss Lewis?"

"Yes." Belle shook his hand.

"You look familiar. Have we met somewhere? The yacht club, maybe? The commodores' dinner dance last year, perhaps?"

"No, I'm from Boston." Belle could feel a bead of nervous sweat forming at her hairline.

"Really? I could have sworn I've seen you before. I do get the Boston paper. Maybe your picture was in it?"

"It doesn't seem likely."

"And you're planning to move to Newcastle? What line of work are you in?"

"Ahhh . . ." Belle took a second to focus on Otto Peterman's eyes. "You see, I just lost my fiancé, and—"

"Oh. I'm sorry to hear that," was the uncomfortable reply. "Well . . . I'm afraid I'm going to have to ask you to step off the terrace. Insurance . . . I'm sure you understand?"

"Yes. It was nice to meet you."

Belle and Janice reentered the building. "He's a good boss," Janice said, "but he can be a little short sometimes. I'm sorry to hear about your loss . . . your fiancé." She placed a friendly and consoling hand on Belle's shoulder, an action that made Belle feel even guiltier.

"He's not dead, Janice . . . at least I hope not! He's just . . . gone."

Janice smiled. "Well, I know that can be tough. I've been there myself. And I probably shouldn't stick my nose in where it's not wanted, but my advice is, move on as soon as you can. There are more men out there than you can shake a stick at."

CHAPTER

26

Throughout the ride from the Peterman office building to the renovated loft spaces on Fifth Street, Belle leafed through the real estate sales package, all the while growing more and more uncomfortable. Janice was turning out to be a kind and helpful person, and Belle found herself wishing she could be as generous and truthful in return. *Keep your eye on the prize,* she reminded herself over and over. *You've got to find Rosco.* But the falsehood became increasingly unpleasant.

Matters worsened as Janice eased her Volvo sedan to a stop directly in front of Margaret House. A number of the women were standing on the sidewalk smoking cigarettes. Rayanne was among them. She ignored the Volvo's arrival, keeping her back solidly to the new and expensive auto, but Belle knew her defiant attitude wouldn't last forever. At heart, Rayanne was a candid and guileless person; honest curiosity was as natural to her as breathing.

"I . . . I think this is a . . . no parking zone," Belle stammered, in an attempt to get Janice to pull her car up the street and away from Rayanne.

"Not to worry," Janice said, reaching into her attaché case and removing a five-by-seven-inch card that read Argus Enterprises. She placed the card on the Volvo's dashboard and added, "I know, it's not kosher, but the Petermans have good friends on the City Council. What can I say? It's one of the little perks I get for being an Argus sales rep."

Janice stepped from the car and walked around to the passenger's side. Uneasily, Belle watched Rayanne out of the corner of her eye. When she thought it was safe, she also exited the car.

"Let's take a second and look at the building's exterior details," Janice said pointing across the street. Belle followed Janice's lead while determinedly ignoring the Margaret House residents. She felt like a heel: one of the numerous snooty, well-clad folk who'd consigned the homeless women to nonentity status.

". . . one of the best representations of this particular style of commercial architecture in the city . . ." Janice was saying. ". . . built in 1888 for a sail manufacturer. Look at the way the copper trim has turned green up there near the cornice. And of course the marble frontis is from Vermont. When Argus Enterprises remodeled the interior we found seascapes and sail designs drawn on many of the walls on what is now a floor-through sixth-floor loft. Some of the artwork dates back to the 1890s. The architect in charge decided against covering the designs, so they remain as visible reminders of Newcastle's history. It's my favorite space in the building. I'd buy it myself if I had the money."

"I can't wait to see it," Belle said, stepping forward to cross the street and distance herself further from Rayanne. "How much are you asking for it again?"

Janice followed. "It's very well priced at three hundred and fifty thousand."

Belle resisted the temptation to sputter a loud "Yikes!" instead saying, "And what was the square footage?"

"You have thirty-five feet of south-facing windows, and a sixty-foot depth, so that gives you twenty-one hundred square. It's one of the best bargains in town. The entire building is, actually. This neighborhood is going to be the next trendy spot. Anyone who gets in on the initial offering will have a very solid investment on their hands."

"I read somewhere that this is part of an empowerment zone. Can you tell me about that?"

Janice appeared not to have heard the question; instead, she unlocked the front door, walking briskly to the rear of the building and a large freight elevator. "Of course the carriage is original, but the mechanism has been upgraded to meet modern safety codes." She swung the gate closed. "Let's start with that sixth-floor space I was describing."

When Janice opened the door to 6A, the two women were drenched with a splash of brilliant sunlight. The entire space was open; no partitioning walls, no plumbing, or kitchen fixtures had been installed. The hardwood floors had been sanded and glowed with a new polyurethane radiance. The tinned ceiling had been refinished and freshly painted. Belle blinked in the brightness, then walked to the far wall and studied the ancient sail designs that had been sketched in chalk and graphite.

"These are amazing," she said.

"They really are special, aren't they? We've kept this space completely raw. The architect is hoping it will go to someone with an unbounded imagination."

Belle walked to the expanse of windows. The view spread down to the refurbished waterfront and out toward

Buzzards Bay. Then she looked down at Margaret House and the Saint Augustine Mission and back to Janice.

"Not to be insensitive," Belle began, watching Janice's reaction, "but do you think this neighborhood will turn around as long as there are homeless shelters across the street?"

The question clearly put Janice on the spot. Obviously, she was a woman concerned about the issue of housing parity in Newcastle, but she was also a real estate agent trying to earn a living. Furthermore, she was well aware that her bosses were tough businessmen who wanted the missions closed or moved. She walked over and stood beside Belle.

"It's a good question, and one I'm sure everyone considers when they look at this area. You just happen to be the first person to actually ask me. I'd be less than honest if I told you that I haven't thought long and hard about an appropriate answer."

Belle opted to back off a little. "It actually doesn't bother me in the least. I was more interested in what the real estate industry feels about the situation. To be candid, it can't be good for business."

Janice folded her arms across her chest and looked down at the women in front of Margaret House. "No . . . the people who can spring for three hundred and fifty thousand want things to be a touch less gritty. Would you like me to show you something in a different area of town?"

"No, no, no, I like this very much. I'm going to give it serious consideration. The only thing that would make me a little uneasy would be living in a building such as this and being the only resident. Have other lofts sold?"

Janice seemed to consider both question and reply, then obviously decided not to lie to Belle. "No, Carol, they haven't. We've had very serious lookers, but nothing's gone into contract yet. I wouldn't want to mislead you on that point."

"That must be tough on Argus . . . the Petermans, that is."

"Well, certainly the sooner they sell these spaces, the better off they'll be, but Argus is a well-structured company. They can wait out market lulls."

"Would they try to persuade the missions to move, do you think? Perhaps attempt rezoning?"

Again, Janice was very careful with her words. "Let me put it this way; I think these lofts are fairly priced in today's market. If Margaret House or the Saint Augustine mission opted to relocate, then the residents here would see a quick upturn in the market."

"But then wouldn't it behoove the Petermans to wait, themselves? If the lofts will become that much more valuable . . . ?"

"I really can't answer for them, Carol. I'm only a sales consultant."

Belle pretended to glance at her watch in surprise. "Oh, look at the time! I really should be heading to the train station if I want to get back to Boston before dinner. What you're saying makes sense, Janice, but I wouldn't want to be the first to buy. Perhaps I can come down to Newcastle again in a week or two . . . see how things have progressed, okay?"

"Sure." Janice handed Belle her business card. "Give me a call; we'll set something up. I think you can expect the situation to be quite different in two weeks."

In response to Belle's curious expression, Janice added. "Spring is traditionally a good time for the market. I'm sure the Petermans feel things will begin moving quickly."

As Janice and Belle left the building, Janice said, "I have plenty of time. Why don't I drop you off at the train station?"

"I don't want you to go out of your way."

"It's not a problem at all."

Belle decided it would be easy enough to walk into the station, wait a few minutes, and then take a cab back to where she'd parked her car, so she said, "Thanks, that would be great."

They crossed the street to the Volvo, but before they could open the car's doors, Rayanne shouted, "Belle! I didn't know it was you in that fancy car! What are you doing down here today?"

Belle stiffened and turned to face her. "Oh, hi, Rayanne, how are you?"

"I finished a new poem. Let me get my book. I'll show it to you."

"Ahhh, you know what, Ray, I'm running a little late. Maybe we can do it some other time, how's that?"

An expression like anger flickered across Rayanne's face. "What brings you down here on a Wednesday, anyway?"

All Belle could think to answer was the truth, "I was looking at the lofts across the street."

Rayanne laughed but the sound was hollow. "Sure you were! Those people are going to drive us back out onto the street, just you wait." Again, a probing distrustful look darkened Ray's face. "You're not selling your house on Captain's Walk, are you?"

"You have a house on Captain's Walk?" Janice asked; she didn't attempt to hide her confusion.

"I . . . I . . . really should be getting to the train station, Janice. I can explain it to you on the way." Belle turned back to Rayanne. "I'm sorry to run off like this, Ray, but I'll catch up with you another time, okay?"

Belle jumped into the Volvo and slammed the door before Rayanne had time to respond. Janice slid into the car a moment later.

"What was that all about?" she asked.

"Oh, Ray? I knew her years ago," Belle lied as she latched her seat belt. "When I was married, my husband and I had a house on Captain's Walk. I assume he still owns it. I moved to Boston when we separated. Rayanne worked for the house painter who was rehabbing the home next door. A long time ago . . ."

Janice's tone was sympathetic. "With a trade like that, she shouldn't have ended up in a shelter."

"She fell on hard times," Belle answered quietly, then added, "She's a good person. . . ."

"Did I hear her call you Belle?"

"Old nickname. They're tough to shake sometimes."

Janice laughed. "Tell me about it! My mother called me Queenie until I was seventeen and threatened to wear a crown if she didn't stop."

The ride to the train station was filled with other inconsequential chat. Belle had a strong desire to confide in Janice; her instincts told her it might be the quicker way to determine the truth about the Petermans. But then she recalled Janice avoiding the topic of the empowerment zone. Argus Enterprises—if not Janice—was hiding something. And Rosco was in the mix.

"Thanks for the lift, Janice. I'll be in touch," Belle said as she left the Volvo.

Janice waved and pulled back into traffic as Belle hurried into the station. She found a bank of telephones. Al Lever was on the other end within twenty seconds.

"Where the hell have you been?" he demanded. "I have half the department looking for you."

She reached into her pocket and removed the tissue containing the mud she'd taken from Argus Enterprises' roof deck. She smiled, unable to resist the pun, "I have some dirt on the Petermans. I'll be at your office ASAP."

CHAPTER

27

The basement of Newcastle's police headquarters was divided into three sections: "The Hole," as Al Lever liked to call it, consisting of six cells for detainees; the morgue and medical examination facility, which was strictly the domain of Carlyle; and Abe Jones's forensics lab. Like most of the building, the lab featured only three colors: gray linoleum flooring, institutional-green walls, and stainless steel fixtures. As Abe peered into his microscope, Lever and Belle hung over his shoulders like two hungry vultures. Finally, after placing his four dirt samples under the lens for what seemed like the hundredth time, Jones raised his eyes and swung around on the stool.

"Close, but no cigar," he sighed.

Belle felt her eyes begin to water. "What do you mean, Abe? That has to be the same dirt. It has to be."

"Sorry, Belle, it isn't. Your soil sample's very close to the other three specimens, but it's not an exact match."

"You're sure?" Lever asked, knowing full well it was a

futile question. Jones's analyses were never off the mark.

"There's no mistaking, Al. The matching samples from Adams Alley, the woman at the bus station, and Rosco's Jeep are all strongly organic . . . no sign of pesticides, herbicides, or commercial fertilizers. On the other hand, in the sample Belle brought us, I'm finding significant deposits of soluble potash, molybdenum, and chelated manganese, along with traces of tetramethrin, a chemical often used for garden infestation control."

Belle let out a long sigh.

"But . . ." Jones continued, holding up an index finger, "Don't get too depressed. This sample does help us narrow down the origin of the others, thanks to their similarity. You say the Petermans brought this dirt down from New Hampshire?"

"Right."

"Then I'd have to say the others came from up that way, too, rather than from the Berkshires as I'd first suspected. The specimens are that close in composition."

"But if the Petermans are planting a city rooftop garden," Lever wondered aloud, "wouldn't they be adding all those chemicals? Fertilizer, pesticides, et cetera? We don't exactly have nature working her miracles in the downtown area."

"Absolutely, Al, but the deposits I'm finding in the Peterman sample have been with this soil for some time. They're well integrated. They weren't added after the earth arrived in Newcastle, they've had time to osmose."

"Meaning they would have also shown up in Rosco's tires, if he'd been to the Peterman's New Hampshire farm?" Belle asked, although she knew the answer.

"I'm afraid so." Jones took her hand. "It was a good try, Belle."

"Thanks." Belle looked at her watch and sat on the stool

beside Jones. Exhaustion played heavily on her face. "The *Crier* will be out in twenty minutes. I suppose I should get back to my office so this kook can find me."

"He seems to be able to *find* you wherever you are," Lever said, adding grimly, "I'll go with you."

"He keeps saying no cops, Al. . . ."

"And this guy still maintains he's holding Rosco somewhere?" Jones asked.

"Right."

"There's got to be a way to end-run him," Jones continued. "We're not taking charge of the situation. We're letting him direct the entire show."

"I thought I was the detective here," Lever interjected, "but, okay, Abe, what do you have in mind? Let's have it."

"I don't know, but rather than searching for Rosco, we should be trying to identify this kook. If we find him, we find Rosco." Jones turned to Belle. "This crossword in the box of roses? I mean, how good was it? Are we talking professional quality, or was it strictly amateur time?"

"It was clever . . . well conceived. The use of language was clear and intelligent . . . symmetrical fifteen-by-fifteen grid. Yes, I would have published it."

"So, there's a possibility this guy's a professional crossword constructor, then?"

"I guess . . . no, it's not possible," Belle said, then questioned how she'd jumped to that conclusion so quickly.

"Why not?"

She was about to respond that crossword creators weren't generally considered psychopaths, but Jones spoke before she had a chance to reply.

"Okay, here's what I'm thinking," he said as he stood and crossed to a doorway at the far side on the lab. "Hold on a second." He walked through the door and returned ninety seconds later carrying a large plastic evidence bag. "Rosco told me you inked in a copy of the puzzle we found under the dead woman? It had an Elvis Presley theme, right?"

"Right," Belle said as her brow wrinkled in confusion. "But it seemed to have no bearing on the situation."

"Maybe. Maybe not. But I'm wondering . . . Is there any way you could connect it to the one you received in the rose box? Or the one on your dashboard? Style, language, pet words?"

Belle thought as both Jones and Lever watched her. Finally, she shook her head. "No. I don't remember anything that seemed to connect the one in the *Sentinel* to the two hand-drawn ones. No. If anything, they were devoid of personality. Clever, yes, but not quirky."

"This may be a long shot, Belle." Jones set the evidence bag on his worktable. "This isn't a very pretty sight . . . so tell me when to stop. Sometimes, I get inured to the sight of dried blood and forget that others aren't comfortable with it." He opened the plastic bag as he spoke. "Normally, I wouldn't have saved all of this. I would have taken samples, kept a fragment or two, and tossed the rest. Actually, it was something you mentioned, Al, that originally piqued my curiosity: the Snoopy cartoon. The *Sentinel* hasn't carried the comic for six months. I checked on that."

"So?" Lever interjected.

"Stay with me here. I scrounged through the Dumpster in Adams Alley that morning, pulled out all the newspapers, and checked the date on each one. First off: there were no papers older than March twenty-seventh of this year, and second—" Jones pulled a bloodied section of newsprint from the evidence bag—"this entertainment section of the *Sentinel* is seven months old . . . and the only portion of that paper to appear in the alley."

Lever let out a nervous laugh. "What are you saying? Snoopy did the deed?"

"Well, my original assessment was that the cartoon page might play a part . . . a Comics Killer kind of scenario. Serial murderers are often attracted to titles of that ilk. But our second death didn't follow the theme, so I was left with two newspapers printed seven months apart . . . and a seemingly dead end to possibly random crimes. Unless the date itself is at issue, a reference mark, as it were, to other unsolved crimes . . . However, something else just struck me." Jones unfolded the newspaper as he spoke. "What else is printed on that page of the *Sentinel*?"

"The crossword puzzle," Belle answered quietly.

Abe spread the paper flat. "As you can see, a number of the clues are bloodstained and difficult to determine, but I think I can scrape the paper down enough to read them. I'm guessing—and this is a real long shot—that this crossword and the one in the paper we found under the dead woman *and* the two hand-drawn crosswords were all created by the same person: our suspect. Because, if the perpetrator didn't plant these newspapers, then why were they there?"

Belle thought a moment. "You're eliminating the idea that street people often wad newsprint into pillows—"

"For the sake of argument, yes."

Again, Belle pondered the suggestion. "But those *Sentinel* crosswords were designed by a legitimate constructor, Abe. I know the puzzle editor up in Boston. Well, I've met him, anyway, and this . . . I mean . . . I just don't see this as a plausible theory."

"Why not?"

"You're suggesting that a contributor to a major U.S. daily is both murderer and kidnapper. I simply can't subscribe to that notion."

"Would you mind completing the puzzle, Belle?" Lever asked softly.

She looked at her watch. She stopped short of sighing but felt her level of irritation and tension rise. "I have to get to the *Crier*, Al. I don't want to miss this guy's phone call. If I upset him further, who knows what he'll do next? I'm just really worried about Rosco."

"I know." Lever spoke more firmly. "This is a long shot, Belle, just like Abe said, but we need to check it out. You can do this puzzle in ten minutes, max. Abe and me? An hour, on the short side. Time isn't on anyone's side right now."

Belle looked at Lever in mounting frustration. "I realize that, Al! Some psycho's got Rosco. Playing word games right now isn't the answer."

"You don't know that!"

Belle spun angrily on Al. "The crossword you found under the dead woman at the bus depot followed an Elvis Presley theme. It had *nothing* to do with crime, murder, foul play—"

Lever was also losing his temper. "Rosco is one of my closest friends, Belle, in case you'd forgotten. And I'm all ears if you have other leads you want to pursue."

Belle grabbed her purse. Lever's hand beat a rapid and nervous tattoo on Jones's worktable while Abe watched the two and wondered whether he should step in or wait for them to cool off.

It was Belle who spoke next. "If you still feel this is important, Al, we'll do it *after* I reconnect with this crazy."

Lever nodded but didn't answer while Abe began busying himself with the newspaper he'd removed from the evidence bag, lightly scratching its surface with a broad knife. "Sixty-five-Across: *J. M. Barrie's little lady.* Any ideas, Al?"

Belle stared at the two men in disbelief. "It's Tinker Bell."

Across

1. Gang next door
6. Finishes
10. Don
14. An Astaire
15. Help a felon
16. Fad
17. Outlaw lady
19. Famous cookie
20. ———gland
21. Fog
23. "You———There"
25. Marine snake
27. Watched
31. Michelin, e.g.
34. Mimes
36. Wind dir.
37. Plath novel
39. Totals
40. Glass container
41. Chit
42. Hippy high
43. Secure by lines
45. Magnani film
49. Wildebeest
50. Blue Eyed———
51. Messenger
52. Subject to death
54. Roadside asst.
56. National output, abbr.
57. Multitude
59. Former Met Rusty
62. ———Rooney
65. J. M. Barrie's little lady
69. Bears or Lions
70. Perry battle site
71. Beginning of a logical argument?
72. Rim
73. Divide
74. Gardner and others

Down

1. Catch
2. Lemon add-on
3. Deneuve film
4. Like Lolly Llama?
5. Appear
6. Shower
7. Atty. org.
8. Microorganism
9. One after the prize
10. Penned
11. Jug part
12. Ripen
13. Classic car
18. Break
22. Bro's sib
23. ———Carney
24. Cheer
26. San Diego resort area
28. Fifth Dimension Blues?
29. Stop
30. ———Moines
32. Building support
33. Air, comb. form
35. ———Bunyan
38. In———of
39. Part of 7-Down
42. Baton Rouge camp.
43. Studio formed in 1924
44. Yoko———
45. Beef up
46. Fuming
47. Sign on a door
48. Sculptor Jean
50. ———Paulo
53. Seasoning
55. Questioned
58. 31-Across, e.g.
60. Funny man Johnson
61. ———mensch, superman

BELLA, BELLA, BELLA

62. Consumed
63. ———Beatty
64. ———Hammarskjold
66. Anais———
67. Robert Edward———
68. ———Alamitos

CHAPTER

28

Abe Jones once again used the flat side of the knife to slide the dried and powdery blood he'd scraped from the seven-month-old old *Boston Sentinel* off his examining table and into a fresh evidence bag. Belle tossed her red Bic pen back into her purse. Racing to complete the crossword, combined with a lack of sleep and too much black coffee, had weakened her knees. She dropped onto the stool next to Al Lever's and allowed her head to sag onto her shoulders.

"Well, it sure as hell wasn't designed as a message to me, was it?" Lever said as he studied the newspaper. "What do we have here? BELL STARR, BELLE DE JOUR at 3-Down, THE BELL JAR, 45-Across BELLIS-SIMA, WEDDING BELL at 28-Down, and TINKER BELL . . . We'd better call that editor you mentioned at the *Sentinel*, Belle. Whether this crossword is connected to the murders or not, I want to know who's fixated on you."

Belle stood and walked to Abe Jones's desk. She reached for the telephone as she plunked herself down in his office chair. "Do I need to dial nine to get an outside line?"

"Yes."

Belle allowed *Boston Information* to connect her directly to the *Sentinel*, feeling she no longer had enough energy to write down the number.

"Yes," she said to the *Sentinel* operator, "Could you connect me to Arthur Simon? . . . It's Belle Graham calling . . . Thank you." While waiting for Simon's line to ring, she looked at Lever. "Al, could you bring me that newspaper, please? Or call out the date."

Lever ferried the paper to Belle and rejoined Jones at the examining table. "This is tough on her," he said sotto voce.

"It's tough on us all," Abe responded quietly. "You try to be hardheaded in these situations, keep the macho guard up—especially for Belle's sake—but Rosco's close to all of us. It's not going to be a pretty picture if we don't locate him. . . . And I mean soon."

"Don't remind me."

"Are you planning to contact Boston PD?"

"I don't know yet." Lever rubbed the back of his neck. "I'll wait and see what she discovers. . . . But, to be honest, with all these soil samples you lifted, I don't think our answer's in Boston. If anything, I'll be calling in the State Police. And, as much as I hate to say it, we're looking at a kidnapping here, and possibly the crossing of state lines, so that means the feds."

"Marvelous—"

"Sorry, did I interrupt something?" Belle asked as she replaced the phone in its cradle.

"Shop talk. . . . What did you find out?"

"Arthur Simon's the puzzle editor at the *Sentinel*. That's who I just spoke with. . . ." Belle took a deep breath as she placed the newspaper back on the examining table. "Your suspicions were correct, Abe, this puzzle and last Saturday's were constructed by the same contributor; a man by the name of Zachary Taylor . . . just like the president. That name also appeared in one of the hand-drawn puzzles."

"So, this guy's up in Boston?" Lever asked.

"Not exactly. Simon's been having trouble with this man for some time. It seems he submitted cryptics—good ones—but then became increasingly possessive, arguing over editing styles, et cetera. He'd actually started to become verbally abusive, and Simon began to fear this man's emotions could engender physical violence. . . . To make a long story short, Simon severed his relationship with this Zachary Taylor a little over a week ago. Saturday's crossword was the last Taylor constructed for the *Sentinel*."

"This is our boy then!" Lever made no attempt to cover his excitement.

Belle answered him. "Maybe, Al. But we can't be positive he's the same person who targeted me with those two hand-drawn puzzles."

"At this point, I don't care, Belle. I want to talk to this guy, and I want to talk to him now. Does Simon know where to locate him?"

"All he's got is a P.O. box in Boston . . . Back Bay section. . . . But there's another interesting part. It seems Zachary Taylor was originally a history professor at Dartmouth . . . 'released from his contract' . . . no details given. At least, none to Arthur Simon, but I gather their phone conversations led Simon to believe Taylor had had some sort of mental breakdown." Belle paused. "And we all know where Dartmouth is."

Lever and Jones said, "New Hampshire," in unison.

"So, do we go up there, Al?" Belle asked.

"No. Let me make some calls first. This guy has to be here in Newcastle. He knows your every move."

"Unless Taylor's got help," Abe interjected. "We've got country mud, and we've got Newcastle—"

Belle interrupted. "I've got to get back to the *Crier*. I can't miss this guy's next contact."

Lever held his arms up and out like a boxing referee. "Stop, stop, everyone stop. Belle, we have a serious stalker out there. Maybe two, if Abe's suggestion is correct. You're not going anywhere without me."

"Al, you can't do that! 'No cops,' that's what I was told. Look, I can get to the *Crier* building alone. . . ."

Lever thought for a long minute, then said, "Okay. But you stay put until he calls. Afterward—" he wrote a phone number on a slip of paper and handed it to her—"you call me. Pronto. The dispatcher will find me, no matter where I am. Once you're in the *Crier* building, I don't want you to leave under *any* circumstances. Is that clear?"

"Yes."

"I don't need to make you promise, do I?"

"I'll stay there, Al."

"If he tells you to go somewhere, to make a move of *any* kind, you *must* check in with me first. I'm giving this guy one phone call, and that's it. After that, I'm calling in the feds, and it'll be a whole new ball of wax." Lever glanced at his watch. "Okay, let's go. You'll take a cab. Don't use your car. I'll walk you to the side door." He turned back to Jones. "Thanks, Abe, I'll keep you posted."

Belle stepped into her office and locked the door. She'd spent the better part of the taxi ride looking out through the rear window in an effort to determine if she was being followed. Nothing had seemed out of place. And when she'd reached the *Crier* building, she hadn't noticed unusual pedestrians. The same had held true for the lobby and elevators. In fact, she'd been familiar with all the people she'd encountered.

Belle moved to the far wall and looked through the window at the bank building across the street and the *For Rent* sign in the upper windows, then brought her eyes down to rest on the bank itself. Since it was after three P.M., the branch was closed; the only movement came from a maintenance man pushing a vacuum cleaner over the dark blue carpet. Belle studied him but gleaned nothing from his behavior. One of the bank officers seemed to be working late at his computer terminal.

Two men, she thought; *one nearby and one at a distance . . .* Her gaze returned to the street. There was a dog-walker, a teenager with a skateboard, a pregnant mom pushing a stroller, a pizza-delivery guy. She refocused on the bank. The maintenance man was gone.

Then the phone rang. Belle nearly jumped out of her skin. "Belle Graham speaking."

"Very nice, *Bellisima.* Very nice, indeed. On the first ring. Obviously you've been anticipating my call."

"Where's Rosco?"

"Let's not rush, shall we? 'The world is too much with us; late and soon . . . ' We'll talk cryptics, first. 'Stand by Your Man'? Nicely done. Witty. It just shows what a modicum of inspiration does for some people."

Belle forced herself to calm down. *Remain rational; find Rosco,* she reminded herself. *Keep Taylor talking, keep him on the line. He'll have to reveal something eventually.* "Old Rough and Ready . . ." she said in a slow drawl. "Is that who I'm speaking with?"

"Very good, *mi bella!* I'm impressed. Indeed, that was President Zachary Taylor's nickname. Did your police friends help you identify me, or did you do it yourself?"

"I haven't spoken to the police!"

"Oh, please. 'Ask me no secrets, and I'll tell you no lies.' "

"Where's Rosco?" Belle said, trying to hide the desperation in her voice. "I've done everything you wanted."

"I believe you're right, Bella, it's time to move ahead. But first, you must admit that my puzzles were excellent . . . fully worthy of publication."

"Look, Zachary . . . Mr. Taylor . . . *Professor* Taylor . . . I've spoken with Arthur Simon at the *Sentinel*. You need help. Tell me where you are . . . where Rosco is. . . . We can help you."

"Simon? Hah, you two are growing more and more alike. The all-powerful editors! The gadflies! The mayflies! The ephemerid! You ignore history because you have so little real knowledge, so little respect and ardor for learning. You reference actors . . . *actors* . . . when you stumble upon a word like Jackson, Garfield, Grant, Washington . . . Ford. Not to mention Taylor! How many times must we suffer through sophomoric clues like: *Elizabeth Blank*? Is Old Rough and Ready too difficult? Did you know that during the Mexican War, Santa Ana had twenty thousand troops as opposed to—?"

"Listen, Professor Taylor, I—"

"Don't interrupt me! You'll speak when I say so, and not a moment before."

There was a long silence. Eventually, Belle said, "Are you still there?"

"Yes. Where was I?"

"Presidents."

"Presidents! No, I was discussing idiotic crossword editors! Your father was a professor, wasn't he, Annabella? What does he feel about your chosen career?"

Belle felt chills run up and down her spine. Who was this man, and how long had he been an unseen part of her existence?

Taylor sighed into the mouthpiece. "I'm sorry it's turning out like this, Belle. It was not my original intention. You're a beautiful woman. We could have worked well together."

"What do you mean?"

"Oh, come now, what do you imagine this entire exercise has been about?"

"I don't know."

"Then you're far less clever than I'd given you credit for."

"I—"

"You can't be so dense as to believe that I—" Taylor stopped in midsentence. The line was quiet for a split second, and then Belle could hear sounds of a frenzied scuffle. "Professor Taylor!" she shouted into the phone. "Hello? Hello?"

The receiver fell. Belle heard it bang rhythmically back and forth. The fight it echoed seemed to escalate. "Professor Taylor?" she called out. "Hello?"

"Belle? Are you there?"

She frowned in utter confusion. "Al . . . ? Is that you . . . ? What are you—?"

Lever's voice panted through the telephone line. "Downstairs . . . outside . . . Look through your window. . . . The pay phone . . . He was using the pay phone on the corner. Just like he did when he left that anonymous tip. Belle, we got him! It's over. It's all over, come on down."

Belle walked to her window. At street level she saw

three Newcastle police cars and Lever's unmarked sedan. Four uniformed officers were standing over a prone man whose wrists had been handcuffed behind his back.

"But where's Rosco?" she whispered into the silent air.

CHAPTER

29

"Gus," Lever said for the fourth time, "Gus, Gus . . . talk to me."

They were sitting in The Hole, cell number four to be precise, in the basement of the Newcastle Police Headquarters. The door to the cell was locked, and Abe Jones and Belle sat on metal folding chairs in the center corridor on the opposite side of the steel bars from Al Lever and Zachary "Gus" Taylor.

"I don't have to talk to you," Taylor announced with a self-satisfied smile. "You haven't even read me my rights. I know full well I'm entitled to them."

"I'm sure you do." Lever returned the smile, although his was far more dangerous. "A professor of history, like yourself. I mean, you can probably recite that old Miranda ditty on your own with no help from me, can't you?"

"As a matter of fact, I can—"

"Bully for you," Al spat back. "So, by *inference,* there's no point in my wasting my breath on it, is there?"

Gus didn't respond. Instead, he gazed calmly at Belle, as though her presence there were a happy and festive one. His smile grew.

"Well, you see, Mr. Taylor," Lever continued, "Your *Miranda* rights mean very little in this present situation. The operative line in the statement is this: 'Anything you say can and will be used against you,' blah-blah-blah. But I already have enough on you to put you away for fifty years. Is this beginning to sink in, *fella?* I have all the *evidence* I need. I'm not here to collect *evidence,* I'm here to find a missing person. And if you know what's good for you, you'll start talking, because I'm losing my patience very quickly."

Taylor could see Lever's beefy fists tighten and his forearms bulge beneath his rolled-up shirtsleeves. A line of sweat started to form on Gus's brow as his grin gradually began to dim. "I . . . don't know. I don't . . . know what you're talking about."

"No? We've got two homicides, *Professor,* and we've got a missing person . . . who happens to be this lady's fiancé and a best buddy to the two men now in front of you. I'd say you were in real trouble here."

"I can't help you."

Lever paused, then continued in a frighteningly quiet tone. "I'm not a violent man, Gus, I'm not. I'm not into police brutality, I'm not into slapping prisoners around, and so forth. But you know what? We're either going to find Rosco in one piece . . . or you're going to die . . . right where you sit. Miranda rights or no Miranda rights, and you have my word on that."

Taylor squinted at Lever, noting the icy calm that had settled over his face—that and the fact that Lever outweighed his prisoner by at least seventy-five pounds. "I meant what I said, Lever," he stammered. "I don't know anything about Rosco! I . . . I . . . was only trying to get to Belle. I wanted her to see my work . . . that's all. I wanted to get close to her."

"I'm not buying that for a second, Taylor."

"It's the truth, I swear." Gus's twitchy body hunched forward; he began to whimper.

"Nice performance, but save it for the movies. I want answers, and I want them now; and if I have to squeeze them out of you, I will." Lever stood and moved toward Gus.

In classic good cop, bad cop fashion, Jones stepped up to the bars. His voice was soft. "Don't do it, Al. This guy's not worth losing your shield over." Abe looked back at Belle, who glanced away; her hands had clenched into fists as well; the knuckles were blue white. When she finally spoke, her head was bent and the words barely audible. "It's been seven months since you created that puzzle. . . ." She looked up abruptly but avoided Gus's eyes. "Ask him why he chose to make himself known to me now, Al."

"You heard the lady."

Taylor gazed longingly at Belle. "You were getting married, and I thought . . . I thought . . ." He leaned forward and rolled his shoulders as if trying to raise his manacled hands.

Belle flinched reflexively, then hardened herself. "Did you hurt Rosco?"

Taylor appealed to Lever. "I didn't hurt anyone. I swear I didn't. And I don't know where her fiancé is."

Lever's jaw tightened in frustration. "Let's go back to Thursday night, *Professor*. How'd your 'Tinker Bell' crossword get under Freddie Carson's head in Adams Alley?"

"I don't know."

Lever leaned into the man, and Taylor's thin, alcoholic body suddenly began to quiver.

"Okay . . . I . . . Yes, I put it there."

"And that was after you killed Carson?"

"No! I didn't do it. I swear! Freddie was dead when I found him."

"Don't play me for a patsy, Gus."

"I'm telling you, I didn't kill him! I only put the puzzle there to get her attention." Gus again nodded in Belle's direction as tears began trickling down his stubbled cheeks. "I mean, she never thanked me . . . even after I mailed her a copy with a letter of dedication. . . . I thought she'd be so pleased. . . . With all that media attention about how that other guy had died in Newcastle, and how Belle Graham had helped find the killer . . . 'Cryptics Queen Clues Coppers' . . . and *Personality* magazine . . ."

Lever looked at Belle, who shook her head in denial, confirming she'd never seen Taylor's letter.

"She never wrote back," Gus continued dismally. "I waited. . . . I even tried to call her a couple of times. . . . I'm a scholar, you know, like her father. . . . She should have responded. She should at least have had the courtesy to respond."

"I never received the puzzle, Zachary," Belle said. Her voice was surprisingly gentle.

Lever interrupted. "Let's get back to the alley. If you're claiming you didn't kill Freddie Carson, who did?"

"I don't know. That's the truth, Lieutenant. And I don't have any information on Rosco, either."

Al straightened up and looked at Jones. "You want to change your advice about going easy on this creep, Abe?" Then Lever swung quickly back to Taylor. "I'm giving you a final chance to make nice, *Professor*. Take it or leave it. Life's not going to be so pleasant from now on. I don't want any more whining about how you don't know a thing about the crime scenes. You were there. Logic says you're involved. History, as you know, is full of logical progressions. Cause and effect."

Gus hung his head and began to mumble. Lever barked out a loud "What's that? I can't hear you, *Professor.*"

"I . . . I'd been drinking. I went into the alley to relieve myself." He glanced sheepishly at Belle. "Anyway . . . there was a car down there, so I stopped and waited. To be polite . . . Something was happening, but it was dark; I couldn't see. . . . After a minute, someone got into the car, and raced away."

"What make of car?"

"I don't know. I was blinded by the headlights. It was large . . . a pickup truck or SUV."

"That's not much help, Taylor. We've had that information for days." Lever lit a cigarette and inhaled deeply. "All right," he said through the smoke, "what did you do next?"

"I continued down the alley and found Freddie. He was dead . . . lying on some newspapers. . . . I . . . I lifted up his head, and . . . and then I slid my copy of the *Sentinel* under his shoulders. After that, I ran."

"You've been carrying that newspaper with you for seven months?" Belle interjected.

Gus didn't answer at first. When he finally did, his tone had assumed a childlike naïveté. "It was just the entertainment section."

Belle shook her head in disbelief.

"I . . . I wanted to give it to you. . . . It was my *bell* crossword. . . . But then . . . well, then I thought . . . Freddie's gone, and your boyfriend's a PI, and sooner or later you'd see it. . . . In this town? With your reputation? It seemed so logical. But you didn't pay any attention . . . so I had to contact you again—"

Lever interrupted again. "What about Carson's dog?"

"Kit wasn't anywhere to be seen. I listened, too. I did! . . . I liked that little dog."

Lever was silent a moment. He perched himself on a metal table beside Taylor's chair. "Okay . . . let's get back to that car. Remember, we're looking at a murder here. Unless you can finger this mystery car, and unless we find some corroborating evidence, you're behind bars for a long, long time. So think about it . . . think real hard."

"I'm trying to tell you, I'd been drinking!" Again, Gus gave Belle an embarrassed glance.

"You're asking me to believe you've created all this turmoil just because you have some weird fixation on Miss Graham?"

"I . . . I . . . She never thanked me! She never realized . . . I was . . . I'm . . . I can't help my—"

"And you're asking us to believe you have no idea where Rosco is? That you have no idea who killed Carson? How about the woman behind the bus station? What do you know about that?"

"Nothing."

"Come off it, Taylor! We just picked you up at the same damn phone booth that was used to report her body to the police. Are you trying to tell me that you didn't make that call last Saturday?"

"I don't know anything about that woman."

"How do you explain the newspapers? The fact that her head was resting on one of your crosswords?"

"I don't have any idea! The cryptic was the last I constructed for the *Sentinel* before Simon fired me. . . . It has to be a coincidence—"

"I'm not a big believer in coincidence when it comes to criminal investigations, Taylor. . . . Okay, back to Miss Graham. How did you know where to contact her? You don't own a car. Or did you have help? Was someone else helping you stalk her?"

"No! Everything I've done, I've accomplished on my own." Again, Taylor's face turned smug. "There were only three logical places she might be: her home, office, or her sister-in-law's. . . . I called each one until I found her—"

"And then told her you were holding Rosco."

"I never said that! I only alluded to the fact that her fiancé was missing—"

"How did you know that he was missing if you weren't involved in nabbing him?"

"I saw a man park Rosco's Jeep near the *Crier* building and then jump into a cab. I assumed he was involved in something illicit, but I didn't think he had anything to do with Freddie."

Lever's jaw went slack. He was clearly nonplused. "What man? What man, Taylor? Why the hell didn't you mention him earlier?"

"I . . . You didn't ask me."

Belle and Abe stood and crowded together by the cell door.

"What did this guy look like?" Lever asked, trying to keep calm.

"I don't know for certain. I was a half block away, maybe a little more. . . . He was on the young side. A healthy build, but not one of those muscle-bound guys: work boots, faded jeans. They were dusty. I thought at the time it was dried concrete or perhaps lime. Everyone's spreading lime on their lawns at this time of year. I remember wondering if he was a landscaper."

Lever turned toward Jones. "Did you lift samples of anything bearing that description from Rosco's Jeep?"

"I only dusted the interior for prints. I pulled mud from

the floorboards to check it with the tire mud, but I haven't gone into the seat fibers yet."

"How long will that take you?"

"A couple of hours."

"You on it?"

"I'm on it." Abe turned to leave.

"And get someone upstairs to start checking the cab companies for me, will ya? See if we can find out who picked this clown up at the *Crier* building."

"Right." Jones lifted his clipboard from the folding chair and placed an arm around Belle's shoulders. "We'll find him. Don't worry."

She gave his cheek a light kiss. "Thanks, Abe." Then she watched as Jones hurried through the doorway at the end of the holding area.

Lever refocused his attention on Gus. "I'm still confused. What were you planning to do with all this, Taylor? What did you expect to accomplish?"

"I wanted to work with her. . . ." He began to whimper again. "I wanted us . . . to be close—"

"Two people are dead!" Lever shouted. "A man's been kidnapped. Do you think this is a game?"

"Al . . ." Belle murmured through the bars, "Don't."

Lever let his gaze bore into Gus for a long moment before turning slowly, methodically removing a key from his pocket, unlocking the door, and stepping out of the cell. He looked back, pointed at Gus, and said, "You don't know how close you came, Taylor."

Lever and Belle walked up to the duty desk on the ground level together. "I'm going to put you in a taxi," he said, "and I want you to go to either Cleo's or Sara's. Call me as soon as you get there, and do not leave. I mean it; that's an order. This thing isn't over yet."

"I'll go to Cleo's. I'll call."

CHAPTER

30

Belle paid the cab driver and stepped onto the paved sidewalk across the street from Cleo's house. At four-thirty in the afternoon, the suburban neighborhood was surprisingly quiet: no children playing in the yards, no bicycles, no strollers, no one mowing a lawn or working in a garden, no mailman, and no UPS trucks delivering packages. Only one car passed, and that was the extent of the traffic. Belle looked at Cleo's drive. The sole vehicle was Geoffrey Wright's dented blue pickup truck. She watched the taxi disappear around the bend, and she crossed the street just as Geoff hurried out of the garage and jumped into the truck.

"Geoff . . . Where's Cleo?" Belle walked toward him as she spoke. She tried to paste on a casual smile but felt it lacked authenticity. "And the kids?"

"They're all at the vet's." He turned the key and started the engine. "One of the damn dogs got sick again."

Belle's smile continued to stick to her lips. "Did they say when they were coming back?"

Geoff's reply was a testy. "Look, Tinker Bell, I'm not a baby-sitter, and I'm not a damn message center, either." He put the truck in gear. "I gotta go."

"But—"

"Late . . . they'll be back late. . . . Cleo said something about the emergency animal hospital down south on the interstate. The dog was really sick."

A sudden sense of dread kept Belle immobilized in front of Geoff Wright's vehicle. "When will you be back?" she asked.

"What is this? Beat-up-your-contractor day? I've got another job to bid, and I'm running late. I have a couple of things to take care of, okay? You won't see me till tomorrow." He released the brake and let the truck roll forward. Belle had no choice but to step aside and watch him barrel out of the drive. For the first time, she noticed his New Hampshire license plate.

A cold sweat covered her. *I'll go inside and lock all the doors,* she decided. *Then I'll call Lever.* She hurried toward the house, but as she opened the front door, a sudden thud arrested her. Belle stopped, nearly congealed with fear. A grunt issued through the kitchen opening, followed by the sound of a woman swearing.

"Sharon?" Belle called out in both hope and fear, and Sharon's wide and pleasant brow appeared.

"Hiya, Belle. I didn't hear you come in."

Relief suffused Belle's face. "Am I glad to see you! Geoff told me Cleo was at the vet's. . . . He didn't tell me you were here—"

"That's because he's in a really foul mood today. Nothing but carping and complaints. . . ." Sharon disappeared. Belle heard something metallic bang against stone. "Sorry, Belle, but I'm in the middle of caulking."

With her brain whirring with questions, Belle turned back to the door, closed and locked it, then walked up the stairs to join Sharon in the kitchen. "I'm going to shut the back door. Is that okay with you?"

"Whatever you want . . ."

Belle bolted it, then tested the patio windows to make certain they were also locked. Finally, she walked into the kitchen. Again, the simple fact of Sharon's presence seemed to fill the house with solidity and strength; her large frame was bent double over the newly installed marble countertop as she ran a bead of caulk along the splashboard. The work was exacting, Sharon's concentration complete.

Belle watched her for a moment. Maybe her suspicions about Geoffrey Wright were unfounded, but then again, maybe Sharon could supply a few missing details.

"Geoff told me he was bidding another job," she said.

"Oh yeah?" Sharon seemed wholly disinterested in the news, then suddenly let out an angry "Ahhhgh!" as her heavy body jerked upward. "Dampen one of those paper towels, and hand it to me, will ya, Belle?"

Belle did as she was asked, and Sharon took the towel and wiped a smudge from the marble. "It's a good thing this stuff is water soluble until it dries."

Belle waited until Sharon returned to her caulk gun. "So, Cleo went to the emergency animal hospital . . . ?"

"If that's what Geoff said . . . I've been playing catch-up since I got back, and trying to keep out of Mr. Disagreeable's way. Something's stuck in his craw."

"He said one of the dogs got sick again."

Sharon's shoulders shrugged. Her focus was on the bead of caulk. "If he says so. I didn't see it."

"Can I ask you something, Sharon?"

A noisy scratching at the back door interrupted them;

Sharon jerked her head around. "Don't let that damn dog in here! Please? The warm weather's making them both shed like crazy. If fur gets into this caulk, I'll have to dig it out and start all over again." Her shoulders hunched in frustration. "It's the only thing I don't like about this job: all that yapping. It's enough to drive you nuts. . . ."

Belle opened the door a crack and tried to shoo the animal away. The result was a prodigious amount of barking and whimpering. She reclosed the door, but the noise didn't abate. "I wanted to ask you a couple of questions about Geoff. . . ."

"All I can say is: Stay out of his way till the job here is done. He gets real touchy toward the end of a project."

Conversation halted as Sharon slammed a fresh tube of caulk into the gun and began vigorously squeezing the trigger to build up pressure. Then she hunkered back over the countertop.

Although strongly tempted to confide in Sharon, Belle decided to continue her circuitous inquiry into Geoff Wright. "You've worked with Geoffrey for some time, haven't you?"

"Five years almost. I only do marble and granite, so if he gets a job that calls for tile, butcher block, or a synthetic material, he calls in someone else. Work's been tight recently on account of the cost of the stone. Also, marble's real soft, so a lot of people are staying away from it. Stains too easily."

"Soft?" Belle chuckled companionably. "I don't know about *that*. I remember hitting my head on my grandmother's counter once when I was a kid. . . . I cried for hours."

"Maybe you have to learn not to hit your head."

Belle ignored the jibe. "So . . . you and Geoff know

each other fairly well. . . . Meaning you'd be aware if he were facing financial difficulties?"

Leaning over the counter, Sharon's response was hesitant. "I don't stick my nose in where it don't belong. He has his own life. I have mine."

"Plus the fact that he lives in New Hampshire, and you're in Vermont."

Sharon didn't reply, so Belle tried a more direct approach. "Does he have any feelings about the development going on in Newcastle?"

"I wouldn't know. But I do know that he doesn't like cities any more than I do."

"There'll be plenty of contracting work in those buildings being renovated . . . high-end stuff: marble, granite, the works."

Sharon seemed disinterested, but Belle kept pushing. "Has he ever mentioned the Peterman brothers?"

Sharon let out a frustrated growl. "I need to concentrate here, okay?" She turned her back and abruptly resumed her work.

Belle remained silent, pondering Sharon's and Geoff Wright's relationship. *Geoffrey lives in New Hampshire,* she told herself. *The Petermans own land in New Hampshire. Sharon works for Geoffrey, but not all the time. However, she's clearly an expert mason, and if he secures other projects in Newcastle, she'll be involved. Or . . . Is he trying to cut her out of the deal? Is that the cause of her sudden truculence?*

"Look, Sharon, I'm going to be straight with you. There's a strong indication a couple of real estate developers named Peterman may be involved in a criminal—"

"I don't know anything about this city."

Belle quelled an irritated sigh and tried another tack.

"You're aware that I do volunteer work at the homeless women's shelter . . . ?"

Sharon nodded once but kept working.

"Well, the Petermans own several buildings near Margaret House . . . one of which they're currently rehabilitating into luxury lofts—"

"What does this have to do with Geoff?"

Belle's answer was evasive. "If he were involved with these developers, would you tell me?"

"I'm not my brother's keeper," was Sharon's blunt response.

"I know Geoff's your friend, Sharon. And I appreciate your loyalty, but this is important. A homeless man and woman were—" The words stopped in Belle's throat. She stared at Sharon's broad back, at her spiky hair, her muscled forearms, and man-sized hands. Then Belle's glance moved to the dusty carpenter's pants and scuffed work boots while Gus's description of the person he'd seen driving Rosco's Jeep ricocheted through her brain: *a big man, six foot or more, brown hair . . . white dust all over his clothes.* Dust that Gus had assumed was lime but could, in fact, have been white Barre marble dust. And a woman that could have been mistaken for a man.

Belle's eyes squinted in sudden outrage, but she forced herself to affect an air of calm. "Never mind," she replied easily. "You're right. . . . Geoffrey's business has nothing to do with you." Against all reasonable inner voices that warned her to back out of the room, find an extension and call Al Lever, run to a neighbor's house, anything but remain in Sharon's presence, anger made Belle plant her feet and stand her ground. If this woman knew where Rosco was, Belle wanted to hear it firsthand. "I guess it can be pretty muddy in Vermont at this time of year . . . New Hampshire, too."

"I don't know about New Hampshire, but this is mud season where I live," was the laconic reply.

"Hard to get around, I guess."

"Not with a truck."

"Oh, that's right," was Belle's airy response, "I forgot about the truck." Her tone turned almost wistful. "A sheep farm . . . green grass and rolling hills . . . I assume you and Geoff grow vegetables, too. Do you find it necessary to use artificial fertilizer or—?"

Sharon slammed the caulking gun on the counter. "I don't know about Geoffrey, but I hate that junk! It poisons the groundwater, and if you're out in the boonies, you're totally dependent on your well. These bozos who buy vacation homes and cover every inch of growing space with chemicals: herbicides, pesticides, genetically altered gunk. They're ruining the land for the rest of us! Not to mention our drinking water!"

The back of Sharon's neck had turned a dark and mean red, and Belle gave her time to cool off before resuming her oblique investigation. "It's really a shame about your truck breaking down."

"What?"

"Your truck. It's a shame you're going to face the expense of repairing it. . . . I know it's not easy relying on public transportation, especially traveling from central Vermont to the Massachusetts coast. . . . What is it? Trailways to Springfield? Or is it Peter Pan Bus Lines?"

"I don't remember."

"Of course not. You were probably so upset about your engine troubles you didn't notice the name of the bus company. Maybe you should consider a Jeep. Like Rosco's."

Sharon leapt up, then suddenly lunged at Belle, grabbing for her shoulders but missing as her quarry dodged out of reach.

"Nice move, Sharon! What are you going to do next? Tie me up? Kill me? Wait for Cleo to come home so you can 'borrow' her car? Like you 'borrowed' Rosco's?" Belle squared herself to face her opponent. Her body felt energized with righteousness and rage, as if nothing—and no one—could stand in her way. "Where's Rosco?" she demanded.

"He's alive. Don't worry."

"That's not good enough." Belle spat out the words; fury made her voice steely.

"He's okay," Sharon muttered. "He shouldn't be, but he is. . . . I'm too damn soft-hearted—"

"Did the Petermans put you up to this?"

"Would you stop with the friggin' Petermans! I don't know who the hell they are!"

"How much are they paying you and Geoffrey for this piece of work?"

"Geoffrey? What does that fancy-dan, Ivy League carpenter have to do with this?"

The women stared at each other, momentarily stunned by mutual incomprehension. It was Belle who broke the silence. "You and Geoffrey killed Freddie Carson . . . and the woman behind the bus depot. And you did it under orders from the Peterman brothers."

Sharon's large mouth snorted in derision. "That simp wouldn't know how to squash a friggin' flea! Geoff Wright! Don't make me laugh! I took care of that stew bum! Not Geoffrey! And not your damn Peterman buddies. And I did the old biddy, too. Me! Mr. Ivy League had nothing to do with this!"

Her confession seemed to take Sharon by surprise; she stared at Belle, but the focus of her eyes was inward rather than outward, as if she were revisiting each event. "The old babe pushed me. I pushed back. I didn't mean to hurt her . . . but she kept getting into my face: 'You gotta pay up!' . . . 'Gotta clean up after them sheep of yours!' . . . 'I'm holding the paper on this place!' Yammmer, yammer, yammer. I put out my hand. . . . She went down like a friggin' sack of flour . . . flat on the marble step!"

"Where's Rosco?" Belle demanded, but Sharon merely looked through her.

"And what was I gonna do then? Drag her back into her own home? Leave her for the local cops? And me behind in my rent?" Sharon paused. "So I dump her in the truck and took off for the city. . . . I'm thinkin', lay the old crone on a bed of newspapers and she'll look like a dead drifter. . . . But this bum pops his head up. . . . Friggin' creep sees the whole friggin' thing! He messed up everything . . . him and his stupid dog!"

"Where's Rosco?"

Sharon's heavy body spun back toward Belle. "You're in trouble, girlie."

Belle glared back. "Is he at your farm in Vermont?"

"Wouldn't you like to know?"

"If you've hurt him—" But Belle didn't finish the sentence, because Sharon suddenly sprang toward her while Belle just as swiftly leapt out of reach.

"There was a witness to Freddie's death, Sharon. Another street person. He supplied Homicide with a description—"

"You're lying! Rosco said he found me on accounta my truck. No one saw nothin'! That's what he said; he said two guys saw a truck that only 'looked' like mine—"

"He's a private investigator. Do you think he'd tell you everything he knows? I've seen him be a lot cagier than that."

Sharon's thin lips opened in a silent scream. She fumbled frantically in a drawer at her back until she found a knife, while Belle's right hand flailed on the countertop behind her, reaching the caulking gun.

As Sharon stepped toward her, the front door banged open, and Effie shouted at the top of her lungs, "I did not! Mom! Tell him I didn't do it!"

As Sharon's head spun toward the sound, Belle swung the caulking gun in a sudden arc, smashing it hard into the side of her skull. Sharon's eyes rolled back, and she dropped like a slab of her precious stone.

When Cleo entered the kitchen, Belle was securing Sharon's hands with the telephone cord.

"What's going *on,* Belle?" But before she could answer, Cleo added a pleased, "Wow, she did a great job with the countertop."

All Belle could think to say was, "I'm glad you came home early."

CHAPTER

31

"I have to admit that it's a valiant display of bravery," Sara Crane Briephs announced to Belle. "Your affianced may feel as sick as a dog—no pun intended—but he's certainly evincing an admirable facade."

At that moment, the *Akbar*'s bow nosed into a small ocean swell, and a spray of salt water flew up from Buzzards Bay and lightly coated one of the main stateroom's starboard portals. A prism of red and purple light careened across the large cabin.

"Ah, the ocean," Sara enthused, " 'And the wheel's kick and the wind's song and the white sail's shaking' . . ."

" 'Sea-Fever,' " Belle answered. "I love that Masefield poem, too." In her simple wedding dress, she studied an unruly wisp of hair in the gilt mirror that hung above a nineteenth-century chest of drawers. The more she played with the strand, the less it seemed to cooperate. She scowled at her reflection as she said, "I believe this experience will cure Rosco of his seasickness once and for all."

Sara laughed. "The power of love, my dear? Is that your theory? Or is it the power of feminine persuasion?"

Belle arched an eyebrow. "Wouldn't that be a comforting notion. No, I think Rosco needs to focus on something other than the movement of the boat . . . and if marriage doesn't distract him, I'm afraid nothing will."

"Well, he 'looks like a million bucks,' as they say in the vernacular. One would never guess the dear boy had spent three days cooped up in a damp cellar with nothing but a puppy to keep him company." Sara sighed. "I believe we have Kit to thank for Rosco's safe return. Even that odious woman had a soft spot for the dog."

Belle tried again to tuck the recalcitrant lock of hair in place while Sara looked over her shoulder. "There are more important things in life than a hairdo, dear child."

Belle turned and smiled at the old woman. "You're a good friend, Sara, you really are . . . and you've made our wedding day very special. Rosco and I can't thank you enough for arranging the use of the senator's yacht."

Sara sniffed dismisively as she sat in a large club chair; the mention of her brother always brought an annoyed expression to her face. "Hal may have supplied the *Akbar* for your wedding, Belle, but he certainly was of no help when it came to shedding light on the financial machinations of those distasteful Peterman brothers."

"I'm sure he had his reasons—"

"If you're imagining his reticence involved campaign contributions, I confronted him on that very issue, and he denied it emphatically. I may disagree with my brother's political views, but he's always been a scrupulously honest man. No, my hunch is there's a federal investigation of Argus Enterprises in the works. At least, Hal seemed to allude to the possibility. Although, why he couldn't tell me remains a mystery. To whom did he think I would speak?"

Belle stifled a laugh. "Maybe to me? Or to Rosco or Al?"

"Don't get cunning with me, young lady. That's not the issue, and you know it." Sara sighed pointedly. "Big government's become too hidebound to act efficiently. While Hal palavers in secret about federal investigations, Newcastle's windows are smashed by unsavory characters—"

Belle's interruption was gentle. "But if those 'unsavory characters' hadn't identified Sharon's pickup truck and its Vermont plates, Rosco might not have put two and two together. And if the DA can produce their testimony against the Petermans . . ."

Sara sniffed again. "Miss Annabella Graham, the eternal optimist." Then the forceful tone was softened by a sudden, beaming smile. Sara's grand and patrician face was transformed into doting grandmother. "Good for you, child. I hope you will always retain your rosy outlook. The world would be a sorry place if pessimism won the day."

There was a tap at the stateroom door.

"Yes?" Belle said.

Abe Jones stepped into the cabin and performed a mock salute. "Captain Lancia wishes to inform you that we will be arriving at the designated coordinates in seven minutes' time." Abe looked Belle up and down and let out a low whistle. "Wow. Look at you. . . . *Che bella cosa!* Almost makes a man want to get hitched. . . . Almost." He held up quivering hands. "I'm shaking just thinking about marriage. It isn't contagious, is it?" He then looked at Sara and added an uneasy, "Good afternoon, Mrs. Briephs."

Sara nodded graciously. "It's nice to see you again, Mr. Jones. And how is our groom faring?"

"Just fine and dandy. Says he's never felt better. I wish I

could say the same for the best man."

"I wasn't aware that dear Albert was prone to *mal de mer*," Sara said.

"No, that's not the problem." Jones looked at Belle and cleared his throat. "Ahhh . . . It seems that between Al and Rosco . . . well, they managed to leave the wedding rings at the jeweler's. They didn't figure it out until a few minutes ago. It's probably too late to turn back, but they thought I should check with you."

Belle laughed and shared a look with Sara. "I was wondering when one of them was planning to fess up to that minor item." Belle reached into her bag and removed two ring boxes. "Fortunately, the salesman at Hudson's called me this morning. Here." She handed the boxes to Abe. "Try to make sure they don't drop them overboard."

Jones saluted again. "Aye, aye, ma'am." He turned to leave, but Sara stopped him.

"Mr. Jones," she said, placing her feet squarely in front of her and causing her spine to stretch even straighter, "I don't know if anyone has thanked you properly for all of your hard work. Clearly, this wonderful day would not have arrived so peacefully if it weren't for your dedication."

"Thank you. It's nice of you to say that, Mrs. Briephs. I only wish I could have narrowed down a few things earlier, like the fact that the mud was from Vermont, and it was a pickup truck those two hired thugs spotted in the alley last Thursday. Sharon had marble slabs, not to mention a body, in her truck bed; and the extra weight produced the tire marks I mistook for an SUV, which cost us a day or two. Of course, Rosco shouldn't have gone up to Vermont without telling anyone—"

"Or wasted time pursuing that hideous Gus character,"

Sara interjected.

"But without Gus and his crosswords, our investigation wouldn't have circled back to the homeless shelter and the connection between the two homicides," Abe added.

Belle smiled a glowing bridal smile. "All's well that ends well."

"I hope you will also learn a modicum of skepticism from this experience, young lady," announced Sara. "There are others in the world like Zachary Taylor. Many, I would imagine."

Belle was about to protest, when the *Akbar*'s engines died to an idle, and the string quartet on the aft deck abruptly stopped their rendition of Brahms's Opus 51.

"This must be the spot," Abe said nervously. "I'd better get these rings to *Albert*." He looked at Belle. "Do you know your cue?"

"Relax, Abe, everything's going to be fine."

"Right . . . well . . . *buona fortuna!*"

Sara stood as Abe hurried out the door. "It looks as if some of Captain Lancia's charm has rubbed off on all concerned. Now, dear, would you like me to leave first or walk to the aft with you?"

"I'd like you to walk with me, Sara. You're giving the bride away, remember?"

Sara was silent a moment. "Are you sorry your father isn't here?"

"I have you," Belle answered.

Sara's blue eyes dulled with passing tears. Finally she spoke. "My son Thompson would have been happy to know of our friendship. . . ."

Belle slipped her arm in Sara's just as the quartet began playing "Un Bel Di" from Puccini's *Madama Butterfly*. "I believe that might be our cue."

They stepped from the stateroom, walked through the main salon, and emerged into the bright May sunshine. Rosco was waiting on the fantail with Lever, Jones, and thirty-some guests and family, including Effie, who wore pink patent leather shoes to match her pink organza dress and who seemed almost to levitate with excitement and joy.

Belle started down the improvised aisle, while Kit, who was lying beside Rosco's left foot, remained asleep and wholly oblivious to the fact that this day might be different from any other in the life of a dog.

Across

1. Vegas opener?
4. Lyric ending, part 1
11. Agathe or Anne; abbr.
14. Mr. Jones
15. Baltimore nine
16. Cereal grain
17. Type of wind or will
18. Most expansive
19. Cpl. or sgt.
20. Try another magazine?
22. Prod
24. Three Dog Night hit
25. Fuss
28. Berkshire race village
31. Lyric ending, part 2
35. Roman god
36. Actor Ty
38. Lean
39. Kalihi———, Hawaii
40. Mr. Yale
41. Back muscle
43. Born
44. Directional suffixes
46. Payment method
48. Ms. Peron
49. Penner of lyric
51. Mr. Zimbalist
53. Donald's girl
54. Wise guy?
55. Stuns
58. Prairie wolf
62. Wedding vow
63. More teary
68. Type of iron
69. The big boys
70. Type of fiber, path, or disc
71. Baseball stat.
72. Legal ending
73. Lyric ending, part 4
74. Mr. Beatty

Down

1. Den
2. Ready, willing, &———
3. Hawk
4. Show featuring lyric
5. Swap
6. Letter opener?
7. Diary
8. Corrida cry
9. Part of MV
10. Regard highly
11. Theme of this puzzle, e.g.
12. It may be soft or hard
13. Jacket type
21. Tic-tac-toe winner
23. Pest
25. Scholarly letters
26. Berate
27. Lab burners
28. Awry
29. Flies high
30. Adhere
31. Trios
32. NL home run champ, 1946–1952
33. French student
34. Type of iron
37. Excuse
42. Lyric ending, part 3
45. North or South of Chicago
47. Weep
50. So. Cal. problem
52. Scoot
54. Expanse
55. FDR or Liberty
56. Summer drinks
57. Type of defense

IN FOR A PENNY, IN FOR A POUND

59. Golf tournament
60. Exhaust
61. Mild oath
64. Stock birth? abbr.
65. Orchestra sec.

66. Ensenada uncle
67. Hosp. section

The Answers

KING'S RANSOM

1 A	2 S	3 P	4 S		5 L	6 A	7 I	8 R		9 E	10 T	11 T	12 A
13 E	R	A	S	E	14 I	N	D	O		15 C	R	I	B
16 D	E	V	I	L	17 I	N	D	I	S	18 G	U	I	S	E
19 I	T	O		20 L	N	G		21 A	L	A			
22 T	H	I	S		23 S		24 C	U	D	25 D		26 O	D	O	R	27 S	28	29
30 H	A	R	D	31 H	E	A	D	E	32 D	33 W	O	M	A	N
		34 S	O	L		35 E	A	U		36 R	E	B	A
37 R	38 B	39 I		40 P	T	A	41	42 T	M	43 S		44 N	E	G
45 A	L	L	S	46	47 I	L	L	48	49 A	A	50 A	
51 S	U	S	P	52 I	C	I	O	53 U	S	M	I	54 N	55 D	56 S
57 H	E	A	L	S		58 T	R	A		59 T	O	U	T
		60 U	N	A	61		62 I	R	63 S		64 T	V	A
65 H	66 E	67 A	R	T	68 B	69 R	E	A	K	70 H	O	T	E	L
71 A	G	O	G		72 C	A	R	L		73 E	L	A	T	E
74 T	O	K	E		75 S	P	A	S		76 D	E	N	S

JUST THE BEGINNING

A	R	E	A		D	E	W			R	E	A	D	S
K	I	N	G		E	U	R		D	O	A	B	L	E
A	G	E	R		S	R	I		E	S	S	O	I	N
			E	P	C	O	T		A	C	T	V		
A	S	K	E	R		P	E	S	T	O		E	E	E
L	E	I		O	K	A	R	C	H	E		T	P	S
S	A	L	A	M	I		S	A	T		C	H	I	P
	B	L	O	O	D	A	N	D	R	O	S	E	S	
P	E	E	K		N	C	O		A	V	A	L	O	N
G	E	R		C	A	R	T	A	P	E		A	D	O
A	S	S		E	P	E	E	S		N	E	W	E	R
		K	E	L	P		B	L	I	S	S			
I	C	I	C	L	E		O	O	O		S	E	A	R
R	U	S	H	E	D		O	P	T		E	R	M	A
R	E	S	O	D			K	E	A		X	R	A	Y

NOT DREAMING

1 R	2 O	3 S	4 C	5 O	■	6 C	7 I	8 G	9 S	■	10 D	11 O	12 G	13 S
14 A	N	T	O	N	■	15 A	N	T	A	■	16 A	R	I	A
17 S	E	A	R	S	■	18 P	L	O	Y	■	19 N	A	R	C
20 T	A	L	K	■	21 B	O	A	■	■	22 K	I	L	L	S
23 A	L	L	■	24 T	H	A	T	W	25 E	26 S	E	E	■	■
■	■	27 R	O	L	E	■	28 T	A	Y	L	■	29 O	30 R	■
31 O	32 R	33 S	E	E	M	■	34 A	T	L	■	■	35 G	I	36 G
37 D	A	T	E	■	38 I	39 S	B	U	T	■	40 A	R	T	E
41 E	V	E	■	42 E	E	E	■	43 A	44 D	R	E	A	M	■
■	45 I	N	46 S	47 I	S	T	■	48 S	W	A	M	■	■	■
■	■	49 W	I	T	H	I	50 N	A	D	R	E	51 A	52 M	53
54 A	55 C	56 T	I	I	■	57 B	U	Y	■	58 E	T	R	E	■
59 L	O	O	T	■	60 U	61 S	A	F	■	62 U	S	H	E	R
63 U	S	M	C	■	64 S	U	R	F	■	65 S	T	O	N	E
66 M	A	S	H	■	67 N	E	S	S	■	68 A	S	S	T	S

STAND BY YOUR MAN

¹U	²F	³O		⁴F	⁵M	⁶C		⁷B	⁸W	⁹I	¹⁰T	¹¹W	¹²O
¹³S	A	L		¹⁴R	A	H		¹⁵R	O	T		¹⁶H	A	S
¹⁷A	R	D	¹⁸M	O	R	E		¹⁹O	L	E	²⁰M	I	S	S
	²¹F	A	M	I	L	²²Y	O	F	M	A	N	
²³O	²⁴D	O	R		²⁵A	S	I	D	E		²⁶N	²⁷I	²⁸C	E
²⁹D	E	G	A	³⁰S		³¹E	N	E		³²V	O	C	A	L
³³D	A	Y	T	O	³⁴N	A		³⁵D	³⁶E	A	F	E	N	S
			³⁷H	U	E				³⁸D	N	A	
³⁹E	⁴⁰X	⁴¹P	O	S	E	S		⁴³C	O	N	C	⁴⁴O	⁴⁵R	⁴⁶D
⁴⁷L	I	A	N	A		⁴⁸T	⁴⁹E	A		⁵⁰A	T	L	A	S
⁵¹F	I	L	M		⁵²T	A	M	P	⁵³A		⁵⁴I	D	E	O
	⁵⁵M	A	⁵⁶N	B	I	T	E	S	⁵⁷D	O	G	
⁵⁸O	⁵⁹P	I	N	I	O	N		⁶⁰C	O	R	N	E	⁶¹L	⁶²L
⁶³H	I	S		⁶⁴N	N	E		⁶⁵O	N	A		⁶⁶M	I	A
⁶⁷M	E	T		⁶⁸O	E	D		⁶⁹D	E	W		⁷⁰S	E	W

BELLA, BELLA, BELLA

1 N	2 A	3 B	4 E	5 S		6 B	7 A	8 G	9 S		10 W	11 E	12 A	13 R
14 A	D	E	L	E		15 A	B	E	T		16 R	A	G	E
17 B	E	L	L	E	18 S	T	A	R	R		19 O	R	E	O
		20 L	Y	M	P	H		21 M	I	22 S	T			
23 A	24 R	E			25 E	E	26 L		27 V	I	E	28 W	29 E	30 D
31 R	A	D	32 I	33 A	L		34 A	35 P	E	S		36 E	N	E
37 T	H	E	B	E	L	38 L	J	A	R		39 A	D	D	S
		40 J	A	R		41 I	O	U		42 L	S	D		
43 M	44 O	O	R		45 B	E	L	L	46 I	S	S	I	47 M	48 A
49 G	N	U		50 S	O	U	L		51 R	U	N	N	E	R
52 M	O	R	53 T	A	L			54 A	A	55 A		56 G	N	P
		57 H	O	S	T		58 T		59 S	T	60 A	61 U	B	
62 A	63 N	D	Y		65 T	66 I	N	K	E	R	B	E	67 L	68 L
69 T	E	A	M		70 E	R	I	E		71 T	E	L	E	O
72 E	D	G	E		73 R	E	N	D		74 E	R	L	E	S

IN FOR A PENNY, IN FOR A POUND

1 L	2 A	3 S		4 I	5 T	6 S	7 L	8 O	9 V	10 E		11 S	12 T	13 E
14 A	B	E		15 O	R	I	O	L	E	S		16 O	A	T
17 I	L	L		18 L	A	R	G	E	S	T		19 N	C	O
20 R	E	L	21 O	A	D				22 E	23 G	G	O	N	
		24 O	N	E		25 P	26 R	27 E	E	N				
28 A	29 S	30 C	O	T		31 T	H	A	T	M	A	32 K	33 E	34 S
35 S	O	L		36 H	37 A	R	D	I	N			38 T	I	L	T
39 K	A	I		40 E	L	I		41 L	A	42 T		43 N	E	E
44 E	R	N	S	45	46 I	N	47 C	A	S	H		48 E	V	A
49 W	S	G	I	50 L	B	E	R	T		51 E	52 F	R	E	M
		53 D	A	I	S	Y		54 O	W	L				
55 D	56 A	57 Z	E	S				58 C	O	Y	59 O	60 T	61 E	
62 I	D	O		63 M	64 I	65 S	66 T	67 I	E	R		68 P	I	G
69 M	E	N		70 O	P	T	I	C	A	L		71 E	R	A
72 E	S	E		73 G	O	R	O	U	N	D		74 N	E	D